LEO

EDITED BY AUSTIN P. SHEEHAN

THE ZODIAC SERIES

The Zodiac Series is a collection of twelve speculative fiction anthologies, each focusing on one of the Zodiac signs. The anthologies feature short stories and poems inspired by each sign, and retellings of the various myths behind those signs.

\#

Capricorn Aquarius Pisces
Aries Taurus Gemini
Cancer Leo Virgo
Libra Scorpio Sagittarius

\#

The Zodiac Series has been produced by Aussie Speculative Fiction, and each anthology contains a diverse selection of tales by talented writers from Australia and New Zealand.

I AM LEO

Zoey Xolton

I am the Lion and my constellation is Leo.

My tarot card is Strength; I am a natural born leader and a
dominant individual.

At my best I am passionate, warm-hearted and creative.

At my worst I am stubborn, inflexible and arrogant.

Fierce and warm, like my element: Fire, mine is a Fixed sign.

I appreciate entertainment, excitement, admiration and expensive
luxuries.

However, I dislike being ignored, and not being respected.

I am ruled by the Sun, and am guardian to the seventh day of the
week.

My colours are gold and orange.

About the Author:

Zoey Xolton is an Australian Speculative Fiction writer, primarily of Dark Fantasy, Paranormal Romance, and Horror. Her works have appeared in over one-hundred themed anthologies, with more due for publication! She has recently celebrated the release of her debut short story collection 'Darkly Ever After'. You can find further details regarding her many publications on her website: www.zoeyxolton.com!

Contents:

FOREWORD

Sasha Hanton

Ruled over by the Sun, the fixed fire sign of Leo endows its natives with boisterous energetic qualities. Known for their fierce natures and active personalities, it is little wonder why the fifth sign of the zodiac is represented by a lion.

The constellation of Leo is one of the oldest, and as such, it was known in most ancient cultures. It's brightest star Regulus (Alpha Leonis) means 'little king' or 'prince' in Latin. In other ancient cultures the star also carried a name associated with a Lion.

Ties to mythology for this constellation are varied. With the signs of the zodiac predominantly linked to Greek mythology, the most common story associated with Leo is that of the Nemean Lion. This great beast was the first of Heracles' (Hercules) twelve labours, it could not be killed by any weapon, so the hero had to wrestle with the beast with his bare hands. After killing the lion, Heracles used its claws to skin it and made himself armour from the pelt. From there, it is assumed either Zeus or Hera placed the Nemean Lion into the sky as a constellation.

In ancient Egypt there are multiple links to Leo. During ancient times when the Sun entered the constellation of Leo it would indicate the hottest time of the year, this also noted the times of the annual flooding of the Nile. The ancient Egyptians believed the star Regulus was the Eye of Ra, which in turn links the constellation with Sekhmet the lion goddess who was born from the Eye of Ra. When Ra grew angry with mankind he took his daughter Hathor—who was referred to as the Eye of Ra—from her place on his brow and sent her to Earth in the form of a lion, becoming Sekhmet when she reached Earth. The Great Sphynx of Egypt also possesses the body of a lion.

Whilst often referred to as a masculine sign, there are also strong feminine energies associated with Leo, as can be seen in its link to the Strength card in the Major Arcana of Tarot. Depicting a maiden alongside a lion, the link between the eighth card of the Major Arcana and Leo is clear. Along with a colour palette of bright yellows and reds, the card radiates a strong fiery power. Leos are often described as being fearless, and the card depicts the calm and confident woman closing the lion's mouth.

Strength is represented by the symbol for infinity (or eternal life) placed over the woman's head, her white gown, crown and belt of flowers, and the gentleness in the features of the lion. The gown and adornments give the woman a regal nature, a trait often associated with Leo. And the roses within her belt portray a union of desires and a strength that even wild forces bow before—symbolically Leos are said to be able to charm anyone and anything. In the upright position this card represents the strength to overcome anything, but in the reverse it conveys an abuse of power and a path to discord.

The traits of Leo individuals tend to be widely known and easy to list. They can come off as attention seekers, artistic, extremely self-confident and assured, proud or arrogant. Leos are often either well-liked or envied, and considered to have attractive personalities for the most part. For those born between July 23rd and August 22nd Leo is the constellation that graces them with its influence.

As Cancer's ruling planet is the Moon, Leo's ruling planet is the Sun. Whilst technically not a planet, for the sake of astrology the Sun works as one, governing over Leo. The Sun, in turn, is represented by many masculine Gods, most prominently Apollo in Greek mythology who lends these children of the Sun artistic talents and rich charismatic skills.

Leos tend to walk a line of either great renown or great infamy amongst those who know them, and from their reputations and star sign alone most will claim to know their kind without ever truly knowing them. Through this anthology you will find that there is more to Leo then the regal lion's visage.

About the Author:

Sasha Hanton grew up in the tropics of Darwin, Northern Territory. From a young age, she devoured books and iced coffee, both of which she continues to intake on an almost daily basis. Now living on beautiful Bribie Island in Queensland, her time is split between writing and spoiling her puppy Miley.

Sasha, who has a Bachelor of Journalism from Bond University, has dabbled in the journalistic profession but finds fiction far more fascinating. Her first published work The Short Story Press Collection *draws on her love for a diverse range of genres and passion for short stories. Coming from a multicultural background (Eurasian) she aspires to make her writing inclusive for people from all walks of life and to bring a unique blend of eastern and western culture to her writing.*

Throughout her life, she has been a lover of history and mythology, and at any time will find some way to worm one or the other into her storytelling. When she's not writing or reading she can be found walking her dog and volunteering. You can keep up with her writing over on www.theshortstorypress.wordpress.com

PRIDE

Aveline Pérez de Vera

I cursed as the red double-decker bus disappeared up a foggy Charring Cross Road, shrinking to the size of a keyring, just like those seen on a London tourist stall. Not that swearing has any impact when you're standing alone at the edge of Trafalgar Square at three in the morning wondering how much more loneliness you can endure. The city was in lockdown, and only essential shift workers were likely to be around. No doubt the Dickensian bout of foggy weather obscuring the full moon, as much as the excessively long shift, was contributing to my drained spirits. That, and the empty bus receding on the horizon.

With a sigh I perched on the stone wall by the bus stop, contemplating the length of my wait, legs dangling in a dance of impatience. But a subtle, distant sound interrupted my reverie. A low groan of metal ending with a small pop. Had there been an accident? I glanced at the parked cars up the distant hill near Leicester Square, past the National Gallery. All was still. Had I imagined it?

After all, what is sound, but our perception of noise filtered through our imagination. And tonight, old London town was determined to fuel that imagination. I returned my gaze down the hill hoping to see my bus coming around the roundabout.

Nothing.

Perhaps it was my black mood that made it seem darker. As I surveyed the imperial stone façades of the building opposite, I realised that the streetlights had gone out. I sighed again. Great—a power outage to add to my woes. I hoped the bus driver would be able to see me and stop; if there would be another bus tonight at all.

I returned to my gloomy waiting, musing about strange sounds. The next sound, however, was unmistakable. I have been owned by many dogs over the years, and I know the sound of a tongue lapping water. It came from the symmetrically arranged fountains in the dark centre of Trafalgar Square. When a break in the clouds allowed a little moonlight to reflect off the now silent pools of water, I could make out a shape.

It was large, although hunched over. A surge of adrenalin shot through my body as I conjured up thoughts of escaped zoo animals. I must have gasped, for it sought me out with a curious gaze.

PRIDE

They say you have two options: fight or flight. I had no plan to fight anything, certainly not a six-metre beast, but I stood rooted to the spot. There was no mistaking that flowing mane, the power in the shoulders, the pudgy curve of the cheeks above the soft mouth, and those huge paws balanced on the wall of the fountain. It was a lion; a large bronze lion; a large bronze statue lion. The sort of Lion that usually features in photos of a memorable holiday in London.

Behind the lion was an empty stone pedestal. I glanced in disbelief back to the shimmering beast. My thoughts were not about how a bronze statue could move, but whether a person could be eaten by one. Or was being crushed to death more likely? The slick creature tilted its head to better consider me, and I held my breath until my ears popped.

Only, it wasn't my ears. It was the popping sound I had heard earlier. Through the fog, I could just make out a second lion slamming into the first. My heart stopped, thinking I was about to witness carnage, but the second lion began head-butting the first with more affection than malice. With the first lion's attention diverted, I was happily released from his gaze. As the two cavorted under the watchful gaze of Admiral Nelson, I watched in disbelief. The second lion paused to take a delicate drink from the fountain, allowing the first to affectionately rub its head along his companion's shoulders.

At the edge of my hearing was the low rumble of purring.

The pair were soon joined by the remaining two lion statues. They all looked so similar, and yet the way they played was different. The second lion was fiercer, more warlike than the first who had about him a sense of peace, a patience in watching and waiting. The third lion initiated just as much of the play fighting as the second and was determined to come out on top. The last was continually checking their surroundings between playful tussles. His gaze frequently passed across me; his dismissal a reassurance that I was no threat to himself and his fellow playmates.

I have no sense of how long I stood looking in wonder, no doubt wearing a slack-jawed expression the whole time. The rough and tumble had come to an end, and the third and fourth lions were drinking companionably from the fountain, while the second, with diligence and affection, groomed lion number one. There was such a sense of easy companionship, of love and devotion between them. How long had they been together? I had some dim memory of the statues dating from the mid-nineteenth century, so well over a hundred and fifty years then.

And how long had they kept this secret? Stealing away in the bewitching hour of a full moon to play out of sight from the rest of society. Keeping up a façade—literally—of their resolute separateness and stately serenity for the rest of London to admire. Were they like the long-term incarcerated—forced to find intimacy amongst themselves, or was it inevitable that time and circumstance would see them grow into these relationships?

I had a flash of a memory, a photo of myself as a smiling child, dressed in flared corduroy and straddled across the back of one of the lions, the square squalid with pigeons. But which lion? I tried to recall at which angle the photo was taken, but the tolling of four bells interrupted my thoughts.

The lions, too, heard the sound as it washed over the desolate square, its effect damper than the foggy night air itself. Were they suddenly sad, or was I projecting my own longing for companionship in these strange times? Once back on their pedestals, each looking out to a different point on the compass, they were not even going to be able to see each other. It broke my heart. They were not just prisoners of duty, but also in solitary confinement.

With last nudges of wistful affection, each returned to a pedestal and, with paws outstretched, they solemnly settled on their haunches, the nearest lion briefly glancing at me before looking straight ahead into resolute silence. It was the fourth lion to awaken, but surely he was in the original place of the first?

All caution thrown to the wind, I ran down the hill and made my way past the littlest round police office (capacity: one Bobby), past the slick black railings of the Charring Cross Tube entrance, and stopped below the beast that had given me that last lingering look. It was the fourth lion, my vigilant lion. I proceeded to walk around the base of Nelson's Column looking at each of the lions in turn. I had never noticed before how they were slightly distinguishable from each other—different in their looks just as in manner. I stopped in front of the final lion in my little tour of the square.

Here indeed was the first lion of the night, I was sure of it. They had all rotated places, keeping warm the spot once occupied by another of their kind. I reached up and touched a surprisingly warm bronze paw. Was this their saving ritual to keep a little of each other with them until their next meeting? I turned and leaned my back against the stone pedestal, the sentimentality rising up as I mused on the little taste of forbidden Victorian hedonism that punctuated this pride's solitary duty to Queen and country.

Perhaps the certainty that there are others like you, who will wait for you, is enough to sustain the waiting? I smiled as I looked up, just in time to see another bus disappearing up Charring Cross Road.

About the Author:

Starting her career as a Linguist, Aveline has never veered far from her love of words. Even as a Training Manager her classes were peppered with names designed to entertain the savvy student (Barb Dwyer, Dusty Rhodes, Brandon Cattle . . .). An avid traveller to more than 70 countries, she now balances her wanderlust with work in the serious world of Planning and Projects, so her writing these days is divided between reports, her travel blog, and the satisfying release gained from creating speculative fiction. She recently moved from Melbourne to London, where she lives in an open relationship with her books.

THE LIONS OF DUNSBROUGH CASTLE

Stephen Herczeg

The great façade of Dunsbrough Castle loomed before them as the Pendergast family drove up the main driveway towards the entrance. A large red and gold flag bearing the three lions of England flapped in the light breeze above the ramparts.

First built in the fourteenth century, the castle had been the family home to the Earl of Dunsbrough for all that time, surviving both the Catholic purges of Henry the Eighth and the civil war of Oliver Cromwell. The line of Earls had ridden the waves of disquiet in the south only to prosper and grow in their home in the North East of Yorkshire.

The castle began life as a modest two storey fortification, but as time and technology advanced had been heightened to four storeys, with wings added as the Dunsbrough family had flowered.

The tenth Earl was a close associate of Charles, the Prince of Wales, and had taken up many of the future King's concerns and causes. His home was the epitome of efficiency in terms of power consumption. It was replete with solar panels on every available roof surface, though hidden behind the crenelated balustrades. Additionally, power was also supplied directly to the castle by the large wind farm that lay off the coast of Whitby. Only in the worst of cases did the castle draw from the regular power grid.

The Earl's other causes were the protection and replenishment of threatened animal species. He had taken both a conservationist and a business approach to the problem, by converting the bulk of the Dunsbrough estate into a zoo. The main purpose was to protect already endangered animals and assist with breeding programs to help replenish their species.

The estate was stocked with African lions, tigers of various breeds, several rare varieties of rhinoceros and a number of endangered South American jaguars, ocelots and maned wolves.

Such a cause was not altogether inexpensive. To contribute to the breeding program, the Earl had set up in-park accommodation for a select few. Those who could afford it were treated to remote accommodation in the middle of the open range areas.

It was to this that the Pendergast family had travelled for nearly two hours from Newcastle.

"Ooh, isn't it lovely," said Grace. "Do you think we get to stay in the castle at all?"

"Don't be silly woman," said Ron. "The tickets mention a Stayfari camp, somewhere deep inside the park."

From the back, Louie piped up. He held a little brochure in his hand and read aloud. "The Stayfari camp is situated five miles from the castle and drops the visitor in the middle of the wilds of Africa and Asia. You won't know which way to turn. Lions to the left. Tigers to the right, plus jaguars, wolves, rhinoceros, giraffes and wild dogs."

"Dogs? Why dogs?" Grace asked. "We've got enough flea-bitten mongrels running round the streets back home."

"It says here that they are African wild dogs from the sub-Saharan plains of central Africa. They are endangered cause they attack sheep and cattle herds and are hunted by the farmers."

"Better not attack me then," she said with a giggle.

As they approached the car park to the right of the castle and pulled into a space and stopped, several long necks rose up before them. The tiny heads, several metres above, stared down with interest.

Ron, Grace and Louie all *oohed* and *aahed* at the graceful giraffes standing on the other side of the hedgerow, then watched in awe as they disappeared from view.

"Roxie, Roxie, did you see that?" Grace asked of her daughter seated next to Louie in the back of the car. When there was no reply Louie elbowed her.

"Hey," she said, slapping him with her free hand. Her other hand held tightly onto her mobile phone. The headphones in her ears blocking off any sound from the outside world.

Louie pointed forward, towards his mother's face as she stared back at her daughter with a touch of disappointment.

"I can't believe you missed that," Grace said.

Roxie pulled the headphones out of her ears. "What?"

Grace shook her head and turned back, preparing to leave the car.

Roxie glanced to her smirking brother. "What?"

"Doofus," he replied.

Inside the ground floor of the castle, they were greeted by a khaki clad guide who was all teeth and Geordie accent and introduced herself as Tracey.

"Probably been as close to Africa as we have," Ron whispered to Grace. She sniggered slightly but stopped when Tracey's gaze fell on her

Tracey explained that the Stayfari camp was situated towards the middle of the estate. It featured four self-contained family apartments, with a fully licenced restaurant and a games room to keep them entertained once the day's touring and viewing had finished.

"Oooh, sounds lovely," said Grace, her voice pitching higher with excitement.

"Is the food covered?" asked Ron. When Tracey nodded and smiled, he asked, "And the drink?" Tracey nodded again and Ron smiled widely with a thankful, "Good, good."

Roxie sat in a small chair to one side, engrossed with the online goings on of her friends, the tinny noise of music echoing out of her headphones.

Louie moved across to the large bay windows that looked out the front of the estate. He stood on his toes to look down the hill and managed to catch a glimpse of the roof tops of houses and buildings. Further off in the distance, the sun sparkled off the calm sea, with dozens of huge wind turbines slowly turning in the light breeze. He turned when Tracey's voice piped up. "If you'll come with me folks, we'll head out to your apartment."

Louie walked past his sister and slapped her on the leg. Her head snapped up and a balled fist rose ready to punch him. He innocently pointed to his parents as they followed Tracey towards the exit. Roxie dropped her hand but stared daggers at her little brother all the same. They hurried over and joined their parents.

A corridor led from the reception area that serviced the zoo and accommodation into the heart of the castle. They crossed a wide-open foyer with a mosaiced marble floor and sweeping staircases that led up to the second storey landing.

Grace's mouth dropped open in awe. Louie smiled taking in all the gold trimmings and wondering how many XBOX games he could swap for them. Ron's inner socialist screamed, all he could think was that nobody should own anything like this, it should be broken down and paid to the workers of the estate. Roxie just stared at her phone, oblivious.

Tracey smiled, observing the looks on their faces. The only people that weren't overawed by the trappings of the foyer were those who came from money, which—to be honest—were most of the visitors here. She had been forewarned about the Pendergast's imminent arrival. The mother had won the tickets in a charity raffle, the weekend away was a dream come true adventure for the whole family.

Louie watched with fascination as they followed Tracey through the elegant hallway to the rear entrance, where an old man stood ramrod straight and introduced himself as Smithers, the Earl's butler. He bowed slightly at the hips to the family, in much the same way as he would bow to the Queen.

Grace was overwhelmed at the sight of Smithers wearing a full white-tie ensemble in the middle of the day. Not a crease or any part of his clothing out of place. She held out her hand to shake his. Smithers looked down at the proffered hand for a moment and Tracey was sure he was going to ignore it, but to his credit, the butler took the hand in his own, bent and kissed it lightly.

"Madam," he said. "Welcome to Dunsbrough Castle. I do hope you enjoy your stay in the grounds of our little zoological gardens."

He turned and bowed to Ron. "And you Sir. We serve to please."

Ron blushed. He'd never been treated as anything less than the tradesman he was.

Louie piped up. "Is the Earl here? Will we see him?"

Smithers turned to Louie. A small smile broke across his face as he glanced at the eager boy. "I'm afraid the Earl is away on business at the moment but will return briefly this afternoon before leaving for a charity function in Whitby this evening. The castle staff are helping with the preparations, that's why we are all a dither this afternoon. The rest of his retinue and I will be going with him, so I'm afraid the castle will be rather empty tonight until quite late. The other servants live in the nearby towns," he said, sighing slightly. "I'm afraid it's the sign of the times. Only old dinosaurs like me live here in the castle nowadays."

Smithers glanced at Tracey.

She piped up. "I'll be staying out at the Stayfari resort with you all, just in case there are questions, or you have any needs over the next couple of days." She pointed outside to the large four-wheel drive troop carrier painted in mottled camouflage stripes. "If you would all like to get into the car, I'll have us at the resort in no time."

Ron looked out at the troop carrier. "Car? Looks more like a truck."

"More or less," said Tracey. "It's a converted ex-army Land Rover. The Earl insisted that all vehicles be electric, but also functional. We'll be using this one today and for our safari tour tomorrow."

Smithers opened the door for the family, and they followed Tracey out into the beautifully manicured grounds. Louie ran forwards to the Land Rover and stopped beside it, looking out beyond the fence bordering the gardens. "Awesome."

From where he stood, a wide grassed savannah had been created with sparse copses of trees and a long dirt track that wound its way to the other compound deep in the estate.

Several large grey rhinoceroses grazed along the track. To one side the small herd of giraffes they had seen were strolling casually towards a man-made waterhole. A tight knit pack of wildebeests stood at the water's edge drinking their fill. Not far away a herd of antelope congregated near a small thicket eating the lush grass.

Ron and Grace stepped up next to him and surveyed the area, both wide-eyed and awestruck by the sight.

Behind them Tracey smiled. She never grew tired of such a wonderful view and would happily continue to do so until she retired. "Wonderful, isn't it?"

The family nodded as one.

Grace turned and spied her daughter with her head glued to her phone. "Roxie, for God's sake girl, you're missing all this," she said, waving her hand at the wonders of nature all around.

Roxie looked up for a moment. Took in the various animals then dropped her eyes back to her phone. "It's a zoo. I've seen it all before."

Grace rolled her eyes and shook her head.

The Pendergasts piled into the Land Rover, with Louie sitting up front next to Tracey with Ron and Grace behind them. Roxie took herself to the back and sat with the suitcases, her eyes only leaving her phone when navigating the cluttered interior of the truck.

The Land Rover had the look of an old World-War II troop carrier with three rows of seats and an area for suitcases at the very rear.

Tracey stepped on the accelerator and the Land Rover pulled away with a slight whirring noise from the electric motor. As they approached the heavily barred metal gate leading into the reserve, she pressed a button on the dashboard. The gate clicked open and swung wide, waited for them to pass by before swinging closed again.

Watching the gate swing shut, Louie piped up. "What happens if the electricity goes out?"

"Hmmm. Nothing I suppose," pondered Tracey. "We have our own solar power on the property which is backed up by the National grid in case we run out. We've never lost power in the two years I've been here. Even if the power goes down we have a battery backup system that lasts for over an hour."

"Well that's a relief," said Grace.

The ride across the plains was relatively smooth, but the Land Rover made sure the occupants knew about every hole and rut it found along the way.

As they approached the resort, Roxie finally piped up from the back. "I've got no bloody signal."

Ron turned and smiled at her. "Good. Now you can join the rest of us and admire the view."

The automatic gate opened to allow them entry into the main resort compound. It consisted of several buildings surrounding a central dirt area which was used to park the trucks. Tracey pulled up next to a second, smaller Land Rover which was nestled next to a recharging station. Dropping down from the cab, she connected the cable to the inlet socket before reaching back in to grab the key ring from the ignition and clip it to her belt.

Louie appeared next to her out of nowhere and asked, "How long will that take?"

Tracey's face dropped a little as she said, "All night. This truck is the only one operating at the moment, we used it on a tour earlier and the battery's basically dead. The battery isn't big 'cause we don't have far to drive around the estate, but it takes ages to charge." She indicated the other vehicle. "That's for the restaurant staff. They'll be gone as soon as we've finished eating."

"So, you are stuck with us then," he said.

"Yep, until morning at least."

Moving to the rear of the truck, Tracey unlatched and dropped the tailgate before pulling the family's suitcases down. She pointed to one of the four units that were spread out before them. "That's yours. The key is inside. I'll bring these over in a minute" Hefting a suitcase, Tracey nodded to the larger building directly opposite. "That's the restaurant and games room. Dinner is served between six and eight. You've got a couple of hours. Come over and have a drink if you like. Remember it's all on the house."

Ron stepped over and grabbed a suitcase. "Don't worry about these, we'll handle them," he said. "And thanks, we'll take you up on that offer in a bit." He turned to his children. "Oi, you lot, grab your suitcases you lazy gits."

Tracey smiled.

After a cursory glance around the apartment, Louie went across to the games room. He revelled in the fact he was the only person there and played several games of one-person pool before Roxie sauntered in.

She held her phone up, looking with disgust at the no-signal icon. "There's no signal and not even any bloody Wi-Fi in this place. It's like we're in the third world or something."

Louie smiled at the irony that was completely missed by his sister. "Pool?"

She nodded and picked up a cue. "I'll break."

They played several games before their parents entered, decked out in their Sunday best. Ron nodded to the large pair of doors that led to the restaurant. "Alright, let's see what this place has got to offer."

They joined Tracey at a table large enough for eight and chatted about the adventures planned for the next day. Louie noticed an older couple at a table as far away from the family as possible. The elegantly dressed couple, resplendent with full heads of grey hair, eyed them with disdain and became more and more agitated as a cavalcade of cocktails and champagne made their way to the family's table and down Ron and Grace's throats. As the night dragged on the Pendergast table as a whole became louder, even Tracey let her façade slip and joined in, stopping only before she lost her head completely.

As their dessert was being served, Louie looked over and noticed the couple had disappeared. He asked Tracey about them.

"That would be your only neighbours. Up from London for the weekend. I think they were hoping for a quiet weekend alone," she said and peered around the table, "Don't know why they were expecting that in the middle of a safari park full of animals."

As the family made their way back across the dirt compound towards their bungalow, all four stopped and stared up at the sky. It was a beautifully cloudless night, and they were as far from civilisation as possible in England. Myriad stars shone down on them, more than they had ever seen in their lives. Several lion roars in the distance added a sense of wonder to the occasion.

"Oh, that's beautiful, so serene," said Grace.

"I didn't know there were that many stars in the sky, it's never this clear in Newcastle," said Ron.

Louie pointed up at sky. "Look, a meteor."

They all watched as a bright flare streaked high above them, heading north. Its tail left a bright trail in the sky and they all jumped as the edge of the sonic boom broke the silent night asunder.

"Oooh, that was scary," Grace said. "Now go on, make a wish."

To the survivors, it would become known as the Fall. An unheralded cataclysm the likes of which mankind had never seen. An extinction event similar to that which killed the dinosaurs and triggered an ice age lasting aeons.

For several years, the meteoroid had travelled through the solar system, displaced from its home in the asteroid belt when a comet impacted in a freak meeting of interstellar objects.

Mathematicians would have cringed at the impossible numbers generated from calculating the probability of its subsequent arrival on Earth. Physicists would simply have stated that the gravitational pull of the planet had altered the massive rock's trajectory.

Regardless, the impact was immense. It slammed down on the northern coast of Greenland at supersonic speed, vaporising the ice sheet and throwing up a cloud of steam and dust that enveloped most of the world bringing with it a perpetual twilight that lasted years.

A tsunamic surge radiated out from the crash site and devastated low-lying coastal cities and towns across Europe, North America and Africa. The compression wave from the impact created cyclonic winds that carried destruction across thousands of miles of sea and land. The United Kingdom, Russia and the Scandinavian countries were the first to feel the brunt.

The United Kingdom, where electricity generation had become dependent on wind power to supplement the national grid, paid the price. The turbines reacted to the storm and ramped up production multiple times their capacity. Before they could be shut down the grid was overloaded, blowing nearly fifty percent of the nation's transformers and permanently disabling the network.

Louie was first to rise. He walked out to the reception room and plonked himself down onto the settee. His head throbbed and he struggled to stop the noise of last night's howling wind from intruding on his conscience.

Not long after they'd all gone to bed, the remote roar of the big cats had been replaced by the chainsaw noise from the next room as his father snored into the night.

Then the wind had hit.

A howling tempest rose outside of the little cabin. The wind buffeting the building with such force that Louie was sure it would be ripped from its foundation.

As a toddler he would have rushed to his parents' bedroom, but he was on the edge of teenage hood and such an action felt more embarrassing than the fear of staying in bed. He had simply pulled the covers over his head and tried to block out the noises. Now his brain felt full of cotton wool.

Grabbing the remote he pushed the *On* button for the TV. After a few moments when nothing happened he tried again.

"Bloody heck, batteries are dead," he said, his eyes darting around quickly to check that his parents weren't in earshot. He walked over to the TV and pressed the power button. Again, nothing happened.

Damn. Tele's on the blink.

His rumbling belly diverted his attention to the kitchenette. He stepped over to the well-stocked refrigerator, opened the door and picked out a bottle of milk. He failed to notice that the air wafting from the fridge was cool, but not as cold as normal.

Raising the milk to his lips, Louie drank deeply from the cool bottle, putting it back without seeing that the light was out. He glanced at the windows, noticing the dull light intruding from outside.

Louie checked his watch. The time was well past seven o'clock. Confused he stepped over to the window and raised the blind. Instead of being bathed in brilliant light a pall of twilight filtered in.

Ah, what a crappy day. Hoped it would be bright and sunny.

Roxie wandered out of the bedroom. Her hair a mess, making her look like she'd been attacked by birds.

Louie smiled. "Nice hair. Do you rent it out to sparrows?"

Roxie made a beeline towards her phone, picking it up and turning it on in one movement. As she waited for it to reboot, she looked towards the window. "What was up with that wind last night? I thought Dad's snoring was bad enough. Then I thought this place was going to blow away."

When Louie shrugged, she turned back and took on her favourite pose of staring down at her screen. The splash screen showed up, then a warning that there was no signal.

"What the hell?" she said louder than needed.

"Boyfriend hasn't texted back?" asked Louie.

"No idiot, still no signal." The low battery sign icon flashed up to annoy her further, the charge indicated it was at five percent. Swearing under her breath, Roxie plugged the cable back into her phone and flicked the switch on and off for the charger. Her phone stubbornly refused to charge. Frustrated, she looked at Louie. "Where's your charger?"

"In my bag. Didn't need my tablet. Too much other stuff to look at."

"Get it," she demanded.

"Piss off."

"Get your charger. I need it," Roxie said, her volume rising.

"No. You can't make me."

"Mum," shouted Roxie.

Within moments a haggard looking Grace staggered out, her eyes half opened from lack of sleep, one hand holding her thumping head. "What the heck is going on?" she asked.

"Doofus here won't give me his charger," Roxie said, her hands firmly on her hips.

"You didn't say please," Louie said, a suppressed grin on his lips.

Roxie turned, her eyes wide in anger, her mouth agape. She looked back at Grace her hands upturned in a questioning pose.

"Well did you?" asked Grace.

"No, but . . ."

"Say please."

Deflated and angry, Roxie turned back towards Louie, drew in a deep breath and slowly said, "Please."

"Sure," said Louie and quickly moved into the bedroom, returning moments later with his tablet charger. He plugged it in, switched it on and gave the cable to Roxie.

She plugged her phone in and watched. Nothing. "Fuck."

"Hey," said Grace. "There's no need for language like that."

"But, this one doesn't work either," she said on the verge of tears.

Louie glanced up at the lights before stepping over to the switch. He flicked it a couple of times. "It's the electricity, it's out."

"Fucking great," said Roxie.

"Oi," came a deeper voice from the bedroom entrance. Ron stepped into the room, he looked like death warmed up, his eyes glazed, his head hanging down. "This is not a factory floor, it's a nice hotel in a castle estate, have some decorum, ay."

He staggered over to Grace and managed to plant a kiss on her forehead. "What the hell was with that weather last night? Sounded like the world was ending. That wind just didn't give up."

"And the animals. The lions roared all night. Must have been afraid of the wind," Louie added.

"I'm surprised you heard anything," Grace said to Ron. "You spent most of the night buzz sawing away."

A sheepish look crossed Ron's face. "Damn was I that drunk?"

When Grace nodded, with a slight pained grin, Ron grimaced and walked across to the window. Pulling the thin curtain aside, he looked out into the compound. "Shit."

"Language," said Grace.

Louie walked over to join his father. "Wow."

The other two joined them.

Outside the compound was a mess. The roof had been stripped from the restaurant building. Several tree branches had slammed against the windows, smashing the glass on impact. Leaves, branches, rubbish and refuse littered the dirt around the truck.

"That would explain why the power's out," said Louie.

"Damn," said Ron. "Must be a line down somewhere."

They stood staring out at the compound for a few moments before turning away.

It was Louie that noticed movement across the other side. He pressed against the glass and spied Tracey making her way slowly towards them across the open area. She stepped slowly, turning her head frantically from side to side, searching the area for something.

"What's Tracey doing?" he asked.

Ron and Grace returned to the window and joined him.

"Interpretive dance?" asked Ron.

Grace chuckled.

Roxie flopped down on the settee, still fuming against the world. She put in her headphones and listened to music as the last of her phone's power drained off into the ether.

Tracey slowed down; her eyes fixed on a point off to her right. Without noticing she stepped onto a loose piece of wood nestled on a small pile of detritus. It collapsed under her weight and sent her stumbling forward. Her eyes darted down to the keychain at her belt. She grabbed for it, seemingly to silence any noise. Her head snapped back to her right; her eyes grew wide in horror.

A tan blur appeared, knocking Tracey over and jumping onto her prone figure.

It was a lion. A huge female. It roared in triumph, bared its teeth and clamped down on Tracey's neck. The horrible *crunch* of bones breaking penetrated the thick windows of the apartment, shocking the three Pendergast witnesses to the core. The lion bathed in crimson as Tracey's throat tore open, fountaining blood in all directions.

"Oh, my God," cried Ron.

Grace simply screamed.

Louie stood stock still, part in fascination, part in horror.

Another tan figure darted towards the fallen tour guide. The lioness snapped at the male. Instead of arguing with his mate, he turned towards the sound of screaming and dashed across to the window. His short sprint was stopped by his head impacting with the thick windowpane. It starred in a pattern of radiating cracks that threatened to burst with any further damage.

Ron grabbed Grace and Louie and dragged them back from the window. He dropped the blind and pulled the curtains across, before turning and dragging air into his lungs to settle himself down. Stepping back, he peered through the edge of the curtain, careful not to entice the lion any further. "Good Lord."

Louie recovered slightly and guided his mother to the settee and sat her down next to Roxie. The girl looked at both of them and pulled her ear buds out. "What's wrong with her?"

Louie's face screwed up in anger, he sneered at his sister and spat. "Idiot. There's lions in the compound. Tracey just got ripped apart, and what were you doing, zoned out as usual?"

"Are you having a go at me? What kind of crap are you spewing?" she asked.

"Did you just miss all that?" Ron asked, shaking his head.

Roxie put her ear buds back in. "You're all nuts, you know that?"

Through the gap in the curtain, Ron spied the cottage with the old couple, beyond that sat the truck, still hooked up to the charging station.

We need the truck. If we can make it to the castle we'll be safe.

His eyes fell on Tracey's corpse. The lioness was still ripping parts from the tour guide's chest and feasting on the meat. He grimaced at the sight but noticed the keys on her belt.

Keys.

Movement to his left grabbed his attention. The door to the elderly couple's cabin banged open as the grey-haired man stepped out, yawned and stretched.

Seeing the danger, Ron shouted at him, and waved out the window. "Get back inside."

The older man stared in disbelief at the devastation before him. Anger grew on his face, he stood indignantly with his hands on his hips and stared intently at the ruination. When he finally noticed Ron, he turned and pointed at him. "Did your children do this?"

Ron simply shook his head.

The lion's appearance around the corner shocked the grey-haired man into action. He shouted in terror before retreating back through the doorway. It was too late, as the door started to close, the lion bolted towards the disappearing figure and leapt through into the apartment.

Screams, shouts and roars echoed from the little cabin.

Suddenly the door opened and a figure wearing a pink bathrobe burst from the room and ran across the dirt compound.

The old woman had no idea where to go, she simply ran for her life away from the lion.

The lioness looked up and saw the flurry of pink fly past her. She forgot all about Tracey and set off after the woman. Its muzzle covered in blood, Ron saw the male step through the doorway and take off after his mate.

Ron watched all three disappeared behind the restaurant, before stepping away, a shocked look on his face. "Oh, my God, that old couple. The lions got them." Running to the door, Ron shouted "We need to go now." He looked back at the stunned faces of his family. "Well come on."

"What?" said Grace.

"We need to move now, while the lions are busy. We need to get to the truck and then to the castle."

"No. We should stay and wait," said Grace.

He turned back and placed her hands on his shoulders. "Something's gone wrong. We don't have much food here, it's all in the restaurant. Anyone from the castle will assume that Tracey is looking after us. But she's dead. We're on our own. The lions know we're in here, when they get hungry, they'll get in. I don't want to wait for help that might not come, and I don't want us to end up like Tracey and the old couple."

Grabbing the door handle, he opened it and peered through the crack. Outside the area was clear. The lions had followed the old lady as she ran behind the restaurant.

"Now," he said as he stepped outside.

Confused the other three darted after him. He whispered to each in turn. "Louie, unplug the charging cable. Grace, Roxie just get ready to pile in. I need to get the keys off Tracey."

As Ron turned to go, Grace grabbed his shoulder and said, "Be careful." He smiled and moved away.

Ron peered around and slowly made his way across to Tracey. She lay on her back with her lifeless eyes staring off into the distance. The lion had ripped out her throat and torn strips from her chest and torso. Ron gagged at the sight and struggled to suppress a cough.

His hand to his mouth, Ron knelt down to grab the keys from her belt, making sure not to make any noise. Ron managed to detach the keyring and stood up, before turning and heading towards the truck.

"Dad."

Ron saw Louie standing beside the truck and pointing towards the restaurant. He looked over and gasped in shock. The lioness padded out from the shadows, stopping for a moment and staring at Ron. He broke into a run towards the truck. The lioness chased after him.

"Dad, hurry," came Louie's terrified plea.

"Ron, please run!" Grace yelled.

It was only ten metres to the truck, but Ron hadn't sprinted since high school. The lioness lived on the run. She closed the fifty-metre distance to Ron almost as quickly as he covered the ten to the truck. Approaching the truck, he fumbled with the keys, almost dropping them in his rush. Ron stopped in surprise, his mouth dropped open, as the door sprung open.

Grace peered out from the driver's seat. "Get in, it was unlocked."

Ron piled into the car and slammed the door shut, just as the lioness pounced, striking the metal door with such force that the truck lurched to one side. All four yelled in surprise. Expecting the worst, Ron peered out of his window. The lioness lay on her side, the rise and fall of her chest telling him she was still alive, but unconscious. "I think she knocked herself out."

A hand slapped against Ron's chest. He looked at it, his mind still reeling.

"Keys," said Grace.

"What?"

"Give me the keys." Grace snatched the keys away as Ron held them out. Flipping through them until she found a large key with a Land Rover symbol on it. Just as she started to slide the key into the tumbler, a large tan body jumped onto the bonnet and stared through the windscreen with baleful eyes.

"Shit," yelled Ron.

Grace squealed in terror, dropping the keys in shock. Roxie and Louie in the rear joined her.

The lion gazed into the cabin, its muzzle red and splashed with gore, dripped onto the windscreen. It pawed at the glass, the claws scraping across the surface, leaving deep scratches.

"Grace, get us out of here," Ron growled.

Grace's right hand groped across the floor trying to find the key ring. She glanced up, straight into the lion's face. It bared its fangs and roared. She screamed again and turned away to peer into the dark footwell. A flash of colour grabbed her attention, she reached for it and secured the key ring, bringing it up in triumph.

Quickly jamming the key into the tumbler, Grace turned the truck on. Lights flared across the dashboard, but the electric motor was silent.

"Is it on?" Ron asked.

Grace accidentally knocked the window wiper stalk causing the wipers to move across the windscreen. The lion jumped slightly in shock, then roared and swatted at the wipers. A field of cracks spread across Grace's sight.

Grace gasped and slammed her foot down on the right-hand pedal. The truck leapt forward, knocking the lion off balance. It fell into the windscreen, cracking it even further threatening to shatter and cave in.

"Brake," shouted Ron.

Grace hit the brake, bringing the truck to a sharp halt, the lion grasped for purchase and failing, slid off the bonnet. It landed heavily on the ground in front of the truck's grill. Grace mashed the accelerator pedal again. The truck shot forward, bouncing twice as it ran over the lion.

Louie looked back. The tan body lay still. The lion wouldn't be chasing them any time soon.

The truck fishtailed around as Grace struggled to control it. She eased off the accelerator and searched for their escape route.

When the castle came into view over a nearby rise, Grace headed towards it. The compound's main gate appeared in their way. It was slightly open, but not far enough. Grace pressed the button on the dashboard, but nothing happened.

"Crap, button's not working," she shouted.

"No electricity, Mum," said Louie.

"Ram it," suggested Ron.

"Fine," said Grace, fixing her gaze on the gate and pushing down hard on the accelerator. The gate burst off its hinges as the Land Rover slammed through.

A small herd of giraffe grazing nearby raised their heads as one and sprinted away from the truck. A large rhinoceros sporting a massive horn turned its head towards the oncoming vehicle. It straddled the ruts that formed the road and held its ground as Grace drove towards it. She honked the horn, but the large animal simply watched with ambivalent eyes.

To the right of the animal was the fence, to the left the ground gently sloped down to a little stream that ran through that part of the estate.

"Stupid fucking," Ron muttered as Grace slowed the truck. Ron reached across and smashed his hand down on the horn. "Get out of the way," he shouted.

"You might not want to do that," came Roxie's voice from the back seat.

Ron turned around to stare at her, surprised to even hear her voice. "Why not?"

"School took us to South Lakes last year, they had rhinos too. They reckoned that the rhinos were pretty tame, but don't like loud noises or fast movements. The guide said that a full-grown rhino could destroy one of the trucks without breaking a sweat."

Ron's eyes grew wide as he turned back and looked at the great grey creature slowly chewing its grass and fixing him with a bored gaze. He pointed off to the left. "Just drive round it then. Be careful."

Grace moved the truck forward, gently driving to the left of the animal. The truck lurched with the angle of the slope. Ron kept his gaze on the rhinoceros as they drove past, alert for any shift in its position. He breathed out a sigh of relief when they left it behind them.

They drove without incident for the next few miles. The compound was alive with giraffe, rhinoceros and the herd of wildebeest that congregated around the small waterhole.

An ominous beeping issued from the vehicle. The battery charge light flashed red highlighting the word *LOW.*

"I think we're running out of power," Grace said. "Tracey said it would take all night to charge." The lights blinked out and the trucked rolled for another fifty metres before coming to a complete stop.

"Fuck," Ron yelled.

All four stared around the truck. The only animals nearby were preoccupied with their own lives and weren't paying them any attention. The family now sat in the middle of a wide barren plain. The fence line was a good three hundred metres to their right, the castle loomed ahead, but was still over a mile away.

"We're gonna have to walk it," said Ron. He slowly opened his door, as quietly as he could, and stepped onto the dirt road. He yelled, "Fuck," as his bare foot trod down onto a sharp stone before shushing and berating himself internally.

The others piled out of the car. Grace and Roxie were clad only in slippers but were at least better protected than Ron.

Louie was the only one to have had the foresight to put shoes on.

Ron moved around to the rear of the truck and opened the backdoor. "We need weapons," he muttered to cut off any questions. After rooting around for a few moments he came out with a cross shaped wheel brace, a thin angled jack handle and the jack base. "Not much, but it's all we've got."

After giving the jack handle to Louie and the wheel brace to Grace, he hefted the heavy jack base and pointed towards the castle. "Let's go then."

Wearing disgusted, frightened looks on their faces, the Pendergast family trudged off towards the only offer of safety they could see.

Ron saw Roxie step over to a discarded stick about a metre long. She picked it up and shrugged at him. "I don't want to be unarmed."

Continuously scanning the area, Ron stayed at the rear as the family trekked over the hard-packed dirt towards the last gate before the castle. He held his eyes on the road, and on the herds of animals peppered around them, checking over his shoulder every now and again. The road behind was clear, even the rhinoceros had moved off.

With only a few hundred yards left before the gate, Ron noticed a black and tan dog about the size of a springer spaniel. "Hey, it's one of those dogs." He crouched down and held out his hand, clicking his fingers. "Here pup, come here."

"Ah, Dad," said Roxie, her voice tremulous, "the guides said those are wild dogs. He won't come for a pat, he'll more likely bite your fingers off."

Ron stood up in shock and held the jack before him, waving his arms and shouting, hoping to scare it off.

The dog raised its nose and sniffed before turning and sprinting away.

"Well that did it," said Ron, proud of his efforts to protect his family. A massive roar echoed from a far-off copse of trees.

"I don't think it was afraid of you Dad," said Roxie.

They all stared towards the roar and saw the herd of wildebeest scatter in all directions. The giraffe nearby followed them. Only the rhinoceros stayed where they were, their ears pricked up and they moved their heads towards the source of the noise.

"Lions?" asked Louie.

"I guess so," replied Ron, peering off towards the trees. It was then a large orange and black striped cat emerged from the tree line and padded across the open grassland.

"Oh, God," he said, turning towards the castle. "Run, it's a fucking tiger."

"Dad, don't be stupid," said Roxie, her voice firm, but soft. "You run, it will run after you."

Louie nodded. "Remember the old lady. The lion chased her when she ran."

Ron stopped still; his eyes locked on the massive tiger. All four stood and watched it skirt the copse of trees, before disappearing back into the foliage.

"Ah, fuck, this is getting too hard," said Ron, wiping a hand across his sweaty forehead.

Grace stepped up to him and placed a hand on his shoulder. "It's okay dear, just take it easy. The gate's not far now, we can carry on a nice steady pace and we'll be fine."

Ron nodded, and kissed her on the forehead. "I'm lucky to have your calm head around."

They headed off with Louie in the lead. He held his jack handle in front of him, like a short sword. Roxie walked next to him.

"How the hell do you know so much about animals?" Louie asked.

Roxie shrugged. "I used to be really interested." She peered around the dusty plains. "But I've grown up I suppose. Still kept the knowledge, just don't care as much anymore."

When they were only fifty metres from the gate, Ron noticed movement off to their right, further along the fence. He stopped and peered across the dry ground. A small set of bushes were moving, with no sign of a breeze in the still air.

Grace stepped next to him. "What's wrong?"

Pointing at the bushes, he said, "Those trees, they're moving. Probably just another stupid animal. One of them dogs maybe?" He almost screamed as a tan coloured figure burst out of the shrubbery and darted towards them across the plain. "Shit. Run." He grabbed Grace and pushed her in front as they both started to run.

Louie and Roxie saw the lion race towards them. They turned and bolted for the gate. Roxie kept up with him for a few metres before tripping on her slippers and crashing to the ground, throwing up dust and skinning her knees. Louie circled back and helped his sister back to her feet. She stopped and turned.

Louie cried out, "What are you doing? Run."

Roxie pointed at the small white rectangle lying in the dirt. "My phone," she pleaded.

Ron grabbed her by the shoulders and turned her around. "Stuff your phone. I'll buy another one. Now run."

Roxie ran on, then looked back once more at her phone. The lion had closed half the distance to them, and she cried out and ran for all her might.

Louie reached the fence first and pulled to no avail. "Damn, it's jammed shut." He stared towards the top then climbed its six-foot height without any trouble. Louie reached down and helped Roxie climb up and over, dropping to the ground where they both waited for their parents.

As Ron and Grace reached the fence together, Ron grabbed Grace and hoisted her up the gate. She climbed to the top, the stared in horror as a loud roar arose behind them.

Grace screamed at Ron to climb

The lion was barely five metres away. He turned and saw the lion. Looking back to the top of the gate, Ron shook his head. "It'll have me before I get halfway."

"Mum, come down," said Roxie.

Grace dropped down and stared back through at her husband.

Ron grabbed the silver jack in both hands and stood facing the lion.

"Ron, don't, get over here now. It's too dangerous," said Grace.

"I've only got one shot at this," he said. Watching the lion pace back and forth, Ron realised it was sizing him up and holding back. He hoped the bright silver brace in his hand looked dangerous to the cat.

As Ron watched, waited and hoped, the lion stopped pacing, settled back on its haunches then sprang.

Stepping to the side, Ron swung the jack with all his might.

One of the lion's paws shot out as it passed, its claws raking across Ron's midriff. The jack struck the lion in the side of the head, knocking it off balance, causing it to fall heavily against the gate.

Grace jumped away from the gate and cried out in surprise. The lion rolled over onto its side; the breath burst from its lungs.

Ron stood in triumph for a moment before dropping the jack and grabbing at his belly.

From the other side of the fence, Grace ran back to the gate and shouted, "Ron, no!"

Blood poured through Ron's fingers, utter pain and devastation writ large on his face. As he dropped to his knees and cried out, the wounds opened up further. They were horrific. Blood coursed out of the deep gashes in his stomach, followed by his intestines, spooling out onto the dusty ground.

Ron looked up at Grace. "I'm sorry love. So sorry."

Grace grabbed at the gate, pressing her face as far into the wire as she could. "You don't have to be sorry, my love. You can still climb over; we'll get you an ambulance. Come on, you can do it."

He smiled; his teeth covered with gore. "You always were an optimist." A wracking cough made his body shudder. More loops of intestines spilled out of his gut wound and onto the dirt. "I'm gone, Grace. I love you, always have, always will."

Grace's voice pitched higher as she realised the finality of his message. "No, Ron come on, you can do it."

A snuffle and sudden movement from the lion drove her away from the gate. "Oh, Christ."

The great beast regained its feet and shook its head. It let out a roar to show its dominance and stared at Ron.

He simply gazed at the tan coloured animal and said, "Oh, fuck."

The lion pounced, driving Ron onto his back. Straddling the dying man, it opened its mouth wide and chomped down on his face.

Grace's screams drowned out the sound of bones crunching.

Louie dropped to his knees in shock.

Roxie turned away from the sight. She took a deep breath, relaxed, buried the horror deep in her mind before turning back. Roxie grabbed her mother by the arm and dragged her away from the grisly sight of her husband's transition to lion food. "Come on Mum, let's get to safety. We don't know what else is out here." With the other hand she grabbed Louie and pulled him along with her.

The grand castle doors they had gone through only the day before were unlocked. Roxie pushed one open and helped her mother and brother inside the castle. Spying a settee against a nearby wall, Roxie took them across and sat both down.

"Dad," said Louie as his wide-open eyes full of despair locked on to Roxie's own.

She put a hand on his knee and nodded. "He's gone. Nothing we can do for him now."

"What do we do now?" Louie asked. "Where is everybody?"

The entire ground floor was silent.

Roxie walked away and stepped through a nearby doorway. She returned moments later with two glasses of water. "There's a small kitchen through there, but I think the main one is downstairs. There's a stairway going down at the back. I listened but couldn't hear anybody."

She offered one of the glasses to Louie.

He nodded in thanks and suddenly realised how thirsty he was. He quickly drained the glass and put it on a small table nearby.

Roxie sat next to Grace and held the glass out before her. "Mum, please have a drink."

She put the glass to Grace's lips. The water dribbled down onto her mother's stained shirt. Nothing went into her mouth. "Damn."

Regaining some of his composure, Louie looked around and said, "We should look around and try to find someone."

Roxie nodded and looked at her mother. "Do you think she'll be okay?"

Louie nodded. "Yeah, I think she's gone into shock. I saw it on the telly, when something like—" he struggled to say *Dad*—

"what happens is people's minds can just shut down." He struggled to say anything further without bursting into tears, instead pointed towards the main foyer. "There were staircases out there, maybe someone's upstairs."

They headed into the main foyer. Roxie looked back at her mother, who still sat staring off into the distance. Her eyes wide in shock. Her body unmoving. Roxie dropped her head and followed Louie.

The first storey was a lush affair appointed in luxurious fabrics and furniture. The two children walked across the first-floor landing, oblivious to the expense all around them.

"The castle's got a Duke or a Baron or something doesn't it?" asked Roxie.

"He's an Earl. The Earl of Dunsbrough. If I was him I'd be on this floor," Louie answered.

They headed down the hall, checking every door as they went. The first floor was just as silent and empty as the ground.

"This is nuts. This is a castle. How can it be empty?" asked Roxie.

"Smithers said they were going to a party in town," Louie said. "Or maybe it's their day off. It is Saturday after all."

"Some people work on Saturdays," she said.

Louie shrugged. "We're in the country. Maybe they don't here."

They opened a door into a sumptuous bedroom. A large four-poster bed sat against one wall, with beautiful silk fabric sheets that had not been disturbed since last being made.

"Do you think this is the Earl's room?" asked Roxie.

"Yeah, and I don't think he slept here last night," Louie said as he ran his hand across the bedspread. He picked up a phone on a side table and listened.

"Dead," he said.

Roxie moved to the window and drew back the curtains. The world outside was dark and drab. "Oh, my God."

Outside, the world had changed and would never be the same again.

From the Earl's first floor bedroom they could see the entire countryside down to what had once been the town of Whitby.

The town was gone. Replaced by a flooded plain. The roofs of some buildings poked through the water. The ancient abbey was now just a water-logged ruin. Its walls had collapsed under the onslaught of wind and sea after so many centuries of standing against the elements. The great white towers of the offshore windfarm were gone. Snapped off at the base and flung into the deep.

Roxie's resolve finally broke and she burst into tears.

Louie threw his arms around his sister and hugged her tight. "Hey, we'll be fine. We're still alive. Mum will recover. She's just in shock. Until she does we can stay here, or at least until someone finds us. There's got to be food and water somewhere.

They'll turn the power back on. The adults will fix everything, and we'll be fine. That's what adults do."

"Are you sure?" she asked through another burst of tears.

He patted her on the back. "Yeah, sure I'm sure," he said looking out across the broken world outside.

His eyes were wide in fear and trepidation. *This is the end. No-one's coming. It's just the three of us now.*

About the Author:

Stephen is an IT Geek, writer, actor, film maker and Taekwondo Black Belt based in Canberra Australia. He has been writing for over twenty years and has completed a couple of dodgy novels, sixteen feature length screenplays and dozens of short stories and scripts.

Stephen's scripts TITAN, Dark are the Woods, Control *and* Death Spores *have found success in international screenwriting competitions with a win, two runner-up and two top ten finishes.*
His horror stories have featured in various anthologies including: Sproutlings; Hells Bells; Trickster's Treats #1, #2 and #3; Shades of Santa; Below the Stairs; Behind the Mask; Beyond the Infinite; Beside the Seaside; The Body Horror Book; Anemone Enemy; Petrified Punks; Beginnings; Sea of Secrets, Demonic Carnival; Deep Space; A Tribute to H.G. Wells; What If?; Through Death's Door *and* Coffins and Dragons.

Over forty of his drabbles have been accepted by Blood Song Books; Black Hare Press; Fantasia Divinity and ThingsInTheWell.

Several of his Sherlock Holmes pastiches have been accepted for inclusion in anthologies published by Belanger Books and MX Publishing.

You can catch Stephen at his Facebook page:
https://www.facebook.com/stephenherczegauthor

Firestorm

Emilie Morscheck

Ella saw the smoke first. Heavy grey puffs spreading across an otherwise cloudless sky. A gust of wind brought the tang of eucalyptus oil burning. She was not concerned. The rural fire service hadn't issued any warnings. Ella gathered the rest of the washing off the line, folding each item of clothing and setting it down neatly in the basket.

Her children, Sophie and Henry, chased each other around the yard, oblivious to the changing horizon. Ella heaved the basket onto her hip, dodged her children, and walked down the cracked concrete path to the rear veranda. The wood varnish was sticky in the heat, Ella's shoes leaving dusty imprints.

She slid the glass door open, quickly entering and shutting it to trap the cold air inside. The evaporative cooling had made the floor damp and Ella was careful to maintain her balance as she headed towards the children's bedrooms.

In Henry's room, Lego was scattered across the floor. His cupboard, however, was tidy. Ella returned all his fresh clothes to the drawers, her hands pressing on the torn shirt that he refused to let her throw away, the school socks that were stained brown and his uniform for next week.

Sophie was much tidier than her younger brother. She had her toys stacked in the corner under the window. Ella hung up the school dresses, remembering each stitch that she plunged into the checked fabric. Ella had offered her any variation of uniform that Sophie wanted, but the girl had insisted on having a dress like the rest of her friends. That desire wouldn't last long.

The back door slammed, and Ella proceeded to her own room, taking care to restore all items to their usual place. The television turned on to the Saturday cartoons. Much louder than necessary.

With the morning's chores done Ella picked up her novel and settled into her reading chair in the study.

If it weren't for the children, Ella wouldn't have realized the power had gone out. The television had shut off, leaving them to come annoy their mother. Ella left her book on the reading chair and left to find them some lunch.

Through the kitchen windows, the sky had darkened, with the smoke reaching towards her home. No warning text had come about the fire. She'd left her phone charging on the kitchen bench with the volume turned up on full. Ella unplugged the phone and slipped it into her pocket. She prepared food for the children, keeping her tone calm and her voice gentle. And then she began to pack.

A few sets of clothes for each of them. Family photos. The box with her mother's jewellery. The envelope of money she had shoved into the back of the bedside cabinet.

Ella put them all into the boot of her car. The ashy smell had permeated the garage and was leeching into the rest of the house.

Once the children had eaten, Ella strapped them into the car, Henry secured in his booster seat. Sophie looked confused but did as her mother asked. The engine was running, recycling the cool smoke-free air into the cabin.

Ella had one last look around her home, in case there was anything she'd missed. Everything was perfectly in place. The floor which had been clean that morning now had a coating of grey dust. She pressed her fingers into her palm, knowing every moment she stood there the fire could be getting closer.

She drove as quickly as she felt comfortable away from her home. The smoke was getting denser, obscuring the blue above. Down the street and onto the side road. The highway was half an hour away.

The bush alongside the road glowed, the fire deep within. The heat licked Ella through the windows. Every surface in the car began to heat up. The children were complaining, uncomfortable, but Ella had to ignore them. Her foot pressed onto the accelerator.

The engine groaned. Warning lights flickering on the dashboard. Everything was too hot, and getting hotter. Ella wiped her face. Why hadn't she left sooner when she'd seen the oncoming rage and heat? When she'd smelt the crumbling bush?

She turned a steep bend on the road, the boxes in the boot tumbling and crashing. Henry was crying. Sophie was silent.

Fire leapt across the road through the canopy of the trees as sudden as a flighty kangaroo. Ella slammed the brakes as a branch crashed down, sparks flickering. How had it come so close so quickly? In the flames, a shape emerged. Humanoid and growing. Reaching for the car.

Ella put the car in reverse, her mind searching for escape routes. Her driveway at the end of the street, was no doubt already in flames. Her downhill neighbour halfway down the street was her only option, all other exits choked.

The fiery figure crawled into the bush, alighting a shrub and gripping onto a trunk of a tree. It pulled itself up and then began to race through the vegetation, an angry red monster chasing Ella down.

The children were screaming now. Ella couldn't scream. All she could do was drive.

She stopped in front of the neighbour's driveway, throwing the car back into drive, and crashed through the latched gate, the tires struggling to grip the gravel. Maybe the dam had water in it. Maybe.

The fire rushed along the street as if in pursuit, struggling to slow down to make the bend. Ella could see in the rear-view mirror the open hungry mouth and the hands that consumed all.

The dam was at the bottom of the hill. The summer had been dry, as usual, and the dam was muddy and shallow. But it was all Ella had left.

She stopped the car by the edge and grabbed her children. They'd stopped screaming, the image of the fire stuck in their eyes, mouths open. They all coughed out smoke.

Even though the children were better swimmers than her, Ella made Henry cling to her front and Sophie to her back as she waded into the dam. She went as far as she could stand with their heads above the water. It was dark and cold against her burning muscles. Henry's teeth chattered.

The fire caught up. The figure was larger than before.

Ella watched as it danced around the edge of the dam leaving behind glowing embers and ash. The car glowed white, the metal twisting and collapsing into a melted mass. The fuel tank exploded, spitting sparks.

She didn't know how long they were there in the water, waiting for the fire to die. It only got hungrier, burned hotter, desired more. Oxygen was sucked out of the air. Would there be enough to breathe? The surface of the dam appeared small compared to the fire.

In vain it tried to stretch out across the water towards the family. Ella hugged Henry, water slipping into her mouth as she stepped backwards. She was tied, stuck between the extremes of hot and cold, Sophie's grip slipping. Ella called to her, told her to hang on.

For the monster would have to die. There was nothing left to burn.

In a surge of heat, it burst, collapsing in on itself. The world was dark. Smoke blanketed the world. And everything was gone.

About the Author:

Emilie Morscheck is an Australian author of speculative short stories and novels. While working on her first novel she found the time to study engineering and arts at the Australian National University. Emilie was a participant of the Toolkits Fiction program and a creative editor at the ANU's student paper Woroni. Her works on Wattpad.com have over 50,000 reads. In 2019 Emilie received an artsACT grant to edit her YA fantasy novel 'These Cursed Waters'. *She is a fan of kelpies, selkies and watery graves. @EmillieMorscheck*

TEFNUT'S SUN

Neen Cohen

Tefnut's long slender fingers dangle over the darkened edge of the cloud. The rains obey the smallest of her movements. Her brother is near, his wind brushing against her skin, whipping her rain into storms.

Winds move through her mane; flashes of burnt orange curls catch at the edge of her vision.

Her roars shake the world beneath her, warning the humans. She watches as they scurry, collecting their young from the tumultuous sea and pulling them back to safety.

Winds push the waters into waves. They slam against the golden tight-packed sand.

They aren't all collected.

His body is strong, fighting against the waves and pulling himself to land. On the wrong side of the water. His village is too far away.

"Well he'll be gone soon enough." Her brother Shu's breath whispers on the wind.

"We are to give life, not take it away."

"Oh Tef, we both know life is not all about giving."

"They needed the rain, not the wind or the storm, brother."

He shrugs and departs, leaving Tefnut to grant the earth and its people the much-needed rain. Another roar escapes her open jaws, letting them know the storm is over.

Tefnut smiles as the child, bordering on adulthood, continues to pull himself—despite his waning strength—to a small cave along the rocks.

She feels his heartbeat slow as he lay down in the darkness.

His body stops moving, no breath.

A quick flick of her mane to check her brother was not hiding nearby, she breathes a small sun into her hand and guides it into the still form.

His chest rises again, his body radiating light.

"Tut tut sister." Shu's voice breezes over her body.

"He's strong," she growls. "He will carry my strength with pride and courage."

"And what will you name him?"

"He will be my son, my lion."

About the Author:

Neen Cohen is an LGBTQI and speculative fiction author. She's been published through several publishers including Black Hare Press, Little Quail Press, Camden Park Press, and NBH Publishing. She has a Bachelor of Creative Industries and is a member of the Springfield Writers Group.

Neen lives in Brisbane Australia with her partner, son and fur babies. She loves to roam cemeteries, botanic gardens, and construction sites and can often be found writing while sitting against a tree or tombstone.

Check out her latest adventures and upcoming publications over on her Blog: https://wordbubblessite.wordpress.com

CAVEAT EMPTOR

Emily Siggs

Will opened his eyes to discover he still couldn't see.

A cold, musty breeze seeped into his mouth, nose and lungs, bringing with it the sour taste of dirt. He steadied himself against a wall that materialised helpfully from the darkness. But it was no plastic-plated corridor of Serdran. It was a rough, rotting wall of stone.

Will screamed.

Then, in the gloom before him, two bright blue points of light appeared.

Phew. It's probably a rescue party.

Will stumbled towards them, shuffling his slightly-too-big standard issue shoes past (and occasionally into) piles of rubble. "Here! I'm alive!"

His call echoed back to him.

The lights were encased in a metal object. As he approached them, they shifted a little. Then, they blinked.

"Run!" a voice shouted from somewhere in the darkness. "Draw your weapon!"

The voice was like the scrape of metal—harsh, from a dry, strangled throat that had breathed in smoke, swallowed dust. Will could barely make out the words.

A stream of fire pitched from the darkness to roll at his feet—a burning torch. It illuminated everything in flickering light: the concrete floor disappearing under piles of rubble, traces of the metal skeleton of the ceiling, and the huge metal-clad electric-eyed monster that stood before him.

Will screamed again.

"Draw your weapon!" the voice insisted.

The creature snarled, the hiss of pistons revealing long needles in its mouth instead of teeth.

"I don't have one!" Will shouted back.

A second object flew through the air, landing with a loud clang at Will's feet. A wide, shining saw, spotted with rust, one side with big, uneven serrated teeth, its handle wrapped in stained bandages. Will didn't recognise it, beyond the fact it was a saw. It certainly wasn't for wiring or maintenance, perhaps something like a *sword;* he'd heard those mentioned once, they were used in the old days.

"I don't know how to use that!"

"Then it's time to learn, mate," the voice replied, and out of the darkness swirled a figure, burning in the torchlight. They held another rusty saw in one hand, reflecting the firelight.

Will scrambled away as they stepped towards the monster, snatched the torch off the ground. Long wild hair swung through the air just like the blade.

The monster snarled at her. She snarled back, and threw her torch into the monster's face. It struck with a clang and a burst of sparks. She ducked its jaws, its frenzied tail swish, in a firelight-shadow-filled blur. Was the creature made of electrical wires? Or was that strange reptilian skin?

Ramming the wide-toothed saw between the metal plates on its neck, she sawed back and forth through electrical sinews. The monster hissed, the sound of metal scraping across concrete. Smoke billowed from its back, and dark blood flowed from the wound. As she yanked the saw out, the machine's legs gave way and it hit the floor with a smash that echoed into the darkness.

The figure growled with sharp yellow teeth at the monster's body, now simply lumps of lizard-skin oozing blood between metal plates and sparking wires. Will was now unsure as to who he was more afraid of.

She turned and walked over to Will, sheathing the blade on her back in one fluid movement. Her long sleeves, serrated, gouged black breastplate and long pants were all splattered with blood. Her hair was braided back, practically knotted, and in her asymmetrical face, one eye was brown, the other green. A scar sliced faintly down the centre of the green one, and another along her cheekbone.

She smiled, and her left incisor showed. She extended a bloody, calloused hand. "Rhona Vafara."

Will fainted.

Will woke up to find a pair of mismatched eyes centimetres from his nose and two rusty saws either side of his neck.

"Don't scream again, or I'll kill you."

"Get off me!" He struggled, but her biceps put his to shame and her hips were heavy on his stomach.

"No. You're a spy."

"No, I'm not!" Will continued to wrestle against the brute strength of her arms. "Get off me! You're . . . violating me! Help!"

Rhona dropped a saw and shoved a hand over his mouth. "Emptors follow screaming."

"MmmRrrinGmMMM!"

Rhona sighed and got off him, keeping a saw levelled at his neck and her hand over his mouth.

Will slowly sat up. There was a small fire on the floor between the piles of rubble, which glinted dully with shards of broken glass. An iron pot sat nearby, as did a carrying pack, covered in red dirt.

Then, as if opening a horrible orifice, Rhona took her hand away.

Will kept quiet.

Rhona sighed. "So, how'd you get here?" she asked. "I find you in the Dark Caverns, surrounded by Emptors—"

"The what?"

"Dark Caverns. Used to be called"—Rhona squinted—"Perth Station, but who knows what that means. Dark Caverns. Surrounded by Emptors. You know; big metal lizard monster?"

"Stuff like that is still wandering around out here after the war?"

"Robots don't die, Will. Not unless you kill 'em." She glared at the Emptor's hulking body.

Will tried to breathe silently, watching it. "Are there . . . more?"

"Probably," she shrugged.

Will narrowed his eyes. "How do you know my name?"

"Your identity card. William Former, 18/4/3063, bunk 7102, ID number 120810, huh?"

"You can't look at my ID card. That's illegal!"

Rhona smirked. "Out here, nothing is illegal. Legal, either. I live a nice, peaceful life—"

"Peaceful?"

". . . where nobody and nothing can touch me," Rhona said, wiping the blood off her blades onto her trousers. "So, if anyone, any spy, comes and messes it up . . ."

"I'm not a spy."

"Then how'd you get here?"

Will thought about it. "Last I remember, I was programming an emergency evacuation portal . . . and I fell through."

"You fell through an evacuation portal? While programming it?" Rhona stopped wiping her saw and raised an eyebrow.

"Yeah."

Rhona shook her head, placing the first saw down and picking up the second. "No. That's what they want you to believe."

Even with a second look at the saws, Will couldn't work out exactly what they were, although they reminded him of something. They looked thicker at the top, as if they'd been modified to be heavier, do more damage. Whatever the case, he'd already seen the ugly wounds they gave, and wanted them as far as possible from him.

"You've been brainwashed. You're a spy."

"I am not!"

Rhona slowly placed down the saw. "You say you mean no harm?"

"No! I mean, yes!"

"Then, you'll have no reason to refuse the ritual," she hissed.

Will seized up a little. "What ritual?"

Rhona took a small, heavy dagger from her belt. "Hold out your hand."

He did, slowly, trying to stop it from shaking.

"Other way."

"Oh."

Rhona grasped it and yanked up his sleeve. Her warm, slimy hands left bloody fingerprints on his pale, exposed wrist.

His heartbeat quickened.

Underneath the blood, Rhona's hands were tanned and calloused. She rolled up her own sleeves. A wire poked out of her left arm, protruding just above the elbow.

"There's a wire—"

"Yeah."

Rhona took a deep breath, adjusted her grip on the dagger.

Will began to shake, eyes wide. "Please don't! Don't do it!"

At least it's not a saw.

Rhona raised her dagger and it shone in the firelight. Her eyes were inscrutable. "I will do what must be done."

"Oh God, oh God." Will squeezed his eyes shut.

Nothing. Rhona cackled with ugly laughter. "You don't really think I'm going to cut you, do you? Chop off your hand and sacrifice it to the blood gods? Idiot," she snorted, putting the dagger back in her belt and studying Will's hand. "That'd be barbaric."

"You threatened to kill me five minutes ago!"

Rhona chuckled. "Oh, lighten up."

"Yeah. Hilarious. What are you actually doing?"

"Reading your palm." Her grip was surprisingly gentle.

"There's nothing written on it."

Rhona rolled her eyes. "The Fates are telling me all about you," she said, as if that was far more sensible.

"Fates? Like in those old . . . fairy tales? Ha ha, Rhona. Such a joker. You know, you'd really get it in Serdran for your funny old ways. First the dagger thing, then this . . ." Will chuckled, trying hard to smile.

Rhona stared at Will, lips pursed, eyes narrowed. One brown, one green.

"Uhh . . . you're serious?"

"Yes."

Will shook his head. "Impossible."

"Possible."

She still hadn't let go of his hand. "Made-up."

"Real."

Will didn't think anyone had held his hand before, and he desperately wanted her to let go but also not let go, both at once.

"You think you can tell things about me from my hands?"

"Don't you think your hands show who you are and what you do with them?" Rhona asked.

Will hid his hands in his pockets.

"Guilty conscience, Will?" Rhona smirked. Gosh, that smirk suited her. All lopsided and knowing.

He paused. "No. I've never done anything with these hands to be guilty of. Well, except this one electric door . . . But that's all I do with them. Wire stuff."

"That's all? I bet you eat. Learn weapons training. Shoot any infidel they tell you to."

Will shook his head. "What?"

"You don't even . . ." Rhona's eyes darted downwards.

Will stared at her blankly.

She sighed. "Ya know?"

"No."

"You've never touched yourself?"

"No."

"You've never touched anyone else?"

Will shrivelled up his nose. "Definitely not. We don't . . . touch things in Serdran."

"Never?" asked Rhona.

"Yeah. Because we're supposed to be concentrating on building a city; surviving. We can't go around indulging our . . . feelings." His cheeks burned.

"How do they even police that?"

"There's cameras everywhere."

"Even in the bunks?"

"Of course."

"What about privacy?"

"Sorry?"

Rhona stared. "But . . . come on, Will. You must have feelings."

"I don't think so. Well . . . maybe a bit, once," he whispered, looking determinedly over Rhona's shoulder.

Rhona went and tended to the fire. "It's important to feel feelings sometimes. Otherwise you get all pent-up. Like a boiling cooking pot."

Will shoved his hands deeper into his pockets.

Will returned to the place near the wall where he'd first appeared and looked for the portal vacuum. Yes, there it was, dilapidated, dusty, severely out of order. There seemed to be a line of tell-tale indents where at least ten had been, all in a row. They would have been perfect for the citizens of a small city to get to another instantaneously.

"So, Serdran thinks it's a good idea to have evacuation portals that lead to a radioactive wasteland?" Rhona asked from behind him. She watched, chewing on something.

"It's not supposed to," Will replied. "It needed reprogramming so it could be used in case of emergency, to lead to the safe evacuation point all the others lead to . . . But it hadn't been reprogrammed, got missed by the first maintenance team, I guess, and it still leads here. That's why I was working on it when I . . . you know."

It didn't feel real.

Everything that has happened since is scary and ridiculous and impossible. I'm probably still lying on the floor of the portal centre, passed out, and . . . all of this is just a dream.

"Well, this used to be a busy city," Rhona said. "Imagine it, people coming in and out, all the time . . ."

They looked around at the silent platform and the dark, cavernous roof. From where Will crouched, Rhona seemed even taller, stocky but strong, and she stood like his Cohort Leader; like she was built for the military. Will supposed she was the leader of everything out here.

Leader of everything . . .

Will realised he was getting distracted.

Portal, Will, portal.

"Maybe I can fix it."

"You better," Rhona said. "Otherwise you die out here. I mean, it's lucky the Fates told me not to harm you in your palm, otherwise you'd be dead already. But as it is?" She shrugged at the portal. "I swear, if you're a spy, and you tell them about me . . ."

"I won't," Will said. "Trust me, nobody would believe me. Got any tools?"

"Besides you?" Rhona muttered as she walked away. She called over her shoulder, "I've got a saw."

Will worked on the portal with makeshift tools. Cool air sunk from the ceiling—it reminded him of the circulation systems in Serdran. His eyes were finally used to the dark.

Darkness didn't exist in Serdran. Fluorescent lights owned every hallway. Here, the walls were curtains of blackness covered with rusty pipes.

How long have I been here? Four hours? A day? When will my cohort notice I'm missing?

On one journey back to the camp, he'd taken a wrong turn. Rhona had hissed just like the Emptor, stopping him in his tracks.

He'd looked down to see the platform edge fall into blackness just footsteps away.

"Got that thing fixed yet?"

"No."

"Then come and eat."

Will returned to the camp to find Rhona cooking something black and charred over the fire. She tore off a hunk of whatever it was and took a bite, chewing with her mouth open, her teeth sharp and glinting with saliva.

She eats like a monster . . . I guess that's all she's had to copy.

She stripped the bone bare, her tongue working around it, long and slick. Will wanted to look away, but couldn't.

"What?" Rhona asked, shrugging aggressively before swallowing.

"What's it made of?"

Rhona nodded behind her at the Emptor.

". . . Oh my God."

"Unless you fell through the hole with a bucket of oatmeal, you'll eat what you can to survive."

Will braced himself and started eating. The meat smelled like herbicide. He suppressed his gag reflex. It wasn't so bad after a while.

"Want some more?" Rhona asked when he'd finished.

Will stared.

"More?" Rhona repeated.

Will shook his head. Then nodded. Then shook it again. "Can I?"

Rhona looked him up and down. "They starve you. You're like a stick."

"Not much good cropland."

Rhona shoved some more meat at him. "Eat."

"Will. Get here!" Rhona hissed from the campfire. "Quietly! You know nothing of stealth."

Will hurried over, and Rhona shoved a saw into his hand.

"Battle stations."

There was quiet whirring noise. In the darkness, Will could make out a familiar shape. "Rhona, that's just a utility bot—"

Rhona hit him with her full body weight and Will landed in the dust, the saw's teeth inches from his face. Behind them, something hit a pile of rubble. It cracked and slid in a cascade of broken glass.

". . . that shoots darts," Rhona said, back on her feet.

Will looked up at the thing. The utility bot had long, thin, knife-like claws designed for precision—wiring, bomb-defusal—and springy lizard legs; an organic suspension system. Its body was a metal box with a few vents, and the head, on a slender, flexible neck was a metal cone with no eyes, no mouth, nothing but shining chrome and an open letterbox slit.

"There's . . . other types of Emptors?" Will asked, scrambling off the floor. Tiny, glittery shards of glass stuck on his arms. He held up his saw. Adrenaline turned his mind to sawdust.

Rhona's hand darted out and fixed his grip. "There's more than just Emptors out here," she said, jerking her head up. "And up there. In the light."

Then she shoved him into the concrete again. More rubble fell behind them. "The darts, Will! You take the back of it."

Will ran around the back. He gritted his teeth and slammed the saw into the boxy metal body. It glanced off without even making a dent.

The thing's head rotated full semicircle without moving its legs. Again, the whispering sound of a dart.

"Duck!"

Will dropped as a rusty pipe burst behind him.

Rhona launched herself at the robot, sawing at the its neck. "I've seen cane toads as big as cars and snakes with iron-plated skin . . . giant mechs with antennae like ants."

The bot started to turn its head again.

"Some of them were mistakes, I'm sure. Mistakes they couldn't kill." Rhona dodged the swipe of its shining claws. "They just let 'em loose anyway. Who cares if they kill the enemy?"

The bot locked Rhona's saw in its claws. Rhona struggled against it.

With a whirring noise, it rotated its claws and twisted her saw from her grip, and it crashed to the floor.

"Starglast my guts!" Rhona spat as the bot slashed its blades through her shoulder, tearing through her worn shirt and skin with ease. She hissed, and it sounded exactly like an Emptor. The second claw gouged at her face. Rhona ducked, but the last blade sliced through her left eyebrow. Blood ran into her eye. Screeching so loudly the metal skeleton of the caverns seemed to vibrate, she launched herself at the monster.

Will ducked like he'd seen Rhona do and swiped at the monster's legs with his saw. They tore the skin, and black blood splattered the concrete as the bot stumbled. He manoeuvred around it and smashed his saw into the claws with a metallic crack. He hit it again and again, and one claw broke. It swung, held on by a few wires.

Rhona focused her attack on the side without a working claw and put the robot in a headlock. "Up until a few years ago, I saw new things too," she said through gritted teeth, blood dripping onto the bot's body. The bot tried ineffectually to swivel its head and use its claws. "They were still making military weapons that could think and feel. What's the point of a weapon if you can't control it?"

Rhona bent the bot's neck double, blood pumping rhythmically from her bicep, and grunted as it snapped. "Huh? What's the good in that?"

A small stream of smoke rose from the bot's body, then its legs gave way and it crashed to the ground.

Rhona looked at the smoking heap, then kicked it, her steel-capped boots making a loud dint in the metal. "Gah!"

Will looked at Rhona, then down at his saw. It shone silver, and he could not tell which spots were rust and which were blood. Six of the teeth had sunk through the lizard flesh, and they glistened oily and dark in the firelight. He shuddered and wiped at it, but the blood smudged, staining even more of his hand red. It was still warm. The metallic, eye-watering scent of it mingled with the burning wires.

He took a few deep breaths, but they were full of singed hair and smoke. Rhona warped weirdly as she retrieved her saw, melting through the air, as nausea clawed at his gut. He dropped to his hands and knees and dry-retched.

"Kind of funny, isn't it?" Rhona walked over, kneeled down and patted him on the back.

"Most of Australia decimated; Serdran growing out of a pile of bones . . . only the Emptors and Starglasts and whatever other creatures they cooked up really thrive." Will felt the glass shards slicing into his sticky palms. Rhona's blood dripped onto his shirt. Her voice was perfectly even. "Two sides go to war. The weapons win."

Will forced himself to stand, keeping the contents of his stomach down, and gestured to Rhona's face. "You ok?"

"Yeah. Lucky I don't have to replace this eye again. You?"

Will nodded.

"Thanks for—uh—you know. Stopping it from slicing out my voice box," Rhona said. "Bet it's got wiring tools . . . take them, use them."

Will nodded again. He started picking over the trashed metal.

Rhona sighed. "Well, it's always been this way. And this is the way it's always gonna be."

"What, did the Fates tell you that too?" Will murmured.

"I don't need the Fates to tell me humans will always be shitty."

Will worked on the portal again. It was much easier with the bot's tools.

Beside him, Rhona worked on her shoulder. She pinched the gash together, then pushed a thick, long needle in, drawing white thread through. It came out red. Then she pinched a bit lower, and did it again. Her presence was comforting, even if it was kind of painful watching someone sew their body back together.

While Rhona's here, I'm safe.

And even when they weren't talking, that felt nice too.

I miss my cohort, if this isn't a dream or something, but, Rhona kind of feels like my cohort . . . Even closer, if that's possible. I hope she'll be okay out here when I'm gone.

Will watched out the corner of his eye as the two sides of Rhona's gash pulled together. "Doesn't that hurt?"

"I don't know." She shrugged. A few stitches later, she moved onto the next one. "I'm gonna get some nice new scars to add to my collection."

"What's your . . . uh . . . favourite one?"

Rhona turned around and started taking off her shirt with biceps that bulged. Will opened his mouth to say something, but only let out a tiny strangled yelp as she threw her shirt down.

Will closed his eyes, then opened one of them. Heat flared up in his cheeks. It was the most naked he had seen anyone except himself.

But Rhona's back did not look like his. Her body was a crosshatch of red-pink scars, mostly wild slashes, but nearly half of them were perfect squares and circles, cut with surgical precision. Her muscles were so defined they looked like they were scars in themselves, carved. A grubby piece of green tape held down another wire that stuck out of her right shoulder blade. At the top of her right shoulder, there was a tattoo in fading blue ink, 1036D.

"This one," Rhona said, pointing at a long claw-like curve. It started at her left shoulder, soared down across the dip in her back, shifted with her muscles. It nearly reached down to her wide, stocky hips. "Got it fighting my first Emptor."

Will opened his mouth to reply, but closed it again. He swallowed. Not saying anything felt rude, so he said, "Wow. It's horrible."

"Thanks."

Will shook his head a little. "You look . . . absolutely amazing, it's true—but, um, the regulations state that . . . it's illegal to . . . not that I'm telling you how to live in your own home . . ."

"Am I making you feel things again?" Rhona smirked over her bare shoulder.

Will chose to ignore this question.

Rhona put her shirt back on, then started sewing up her eyebrow like nothing had happened. Soon, four uneven stitches stuck out. Then she started cleaning her sawblades, scrubbing them in silvery, grimy water. Clean now, Will realised what they reminded him of.

"Where'd you get those things? They almost look like medical instruments . . . surgical saws, but . . . far too big."

Rhona looked up, then went back to her work. This time, the sides of her mouth turned down at Will's question. "Why are you so curious? Thought Serdran would've stamped that out. Don't you know what happens to insubordinates?"

"Do you?"

"They feed you to their genetically-engineered monsters."

"That's ridiculous. We don't genetically engineer anything anymore."

"Yeah?" Rhona asked, onto the other saw, scrubbing it hard.

"Big court case five years ago. Containment incident. Monster escaped . . . thirty people died."

Rhona snorted. "You want me to believe you? You're owned by the system."

"How would you know better? You're an insane hermit living off monsters." Will stopped tinkering.

"You're a mutant, aren't you? Your eyes . . ." he said softly.

It was nearly a minute before Rhona blinked.

". . . But I thought they killed mutant babies to stop genetic problems?"

Rhona went back to cleaning the blood off her blades. "Yeah, well. They tried."

"Tried?"

"Where do you think mutant babies and dead bodies go, Will? Let's have a think." Rhona furrowed her brow mockingly. "There's not much safe land in Australia, is there? The safe land is occupied by Serdran. They're not going to take up acres of safe land with graveyards, right? So they chuck 'em into the wasteland."

There was silence for a moment.

"How did you survive?" Will asked gently.

"The Fates saved me."

"No, really." Will stared. Rhona got up.

"The Fates."

"But the Fates aren't—"

Rhona stalked over and held a dripping sawblade to his neck. Cold, grimy water slid from its edge over his Adam's apple and down his chest. "The Fates," she hissed.

"Hey! I've got it working!" Will called. He went and joined Rhona by the fire. "Maybe I'll miss you." He'd wanted to say, 'I'll miss you,' but that wasn't tough enough for Rhona, he was sure.

She snorted.

"Do you have a family?" Will asked.

Rhona jerked around.

". . . I know you think Serdran is scum, and we kill mutants and genetically engineer stuff, but it's not like that anymore. Maybe you could . . ?"

"Could what?"

Will's heart hammered. ". . . Come back with me."

"Yes, I have a family," Rhona muttered. "But I'm not coming with you. Why should I trust your word? They've probably forgotten me anyway. I can't come back!"

"Why?"

Rhona got up and walked over, eyes narrowed. Will looked up at her. With a horrible throaty sound, she spat at his feet. "Put up or shut up, Former."

"What? Oh, here we go. Rhona Vafara, who can only sort things out with her fists."

"Fight me, you coward!" Shadows shifted over her face, her lips, her scars. "You're not in your little city anymore—this is my place! Shut up and fight!"

After a moment, Will stood up. "You call me a coward, but you're just hiding behind your muscles, too scared to tell the truth. You're hiding out here. You're the coward."

Rhona punched straight for his face.

Will ducked. He stumbled out of the way of another flurry of punches. "Come on. Hit me!" he yelled. He was shocked to find he was grinning.

Rhona growled, and it thrilled him.

Nothing like this ever happened in Serdran.

Rhona slammed into Will with all her weight. They crashed to the rubble-covered floor, the concrete flashing towards them then the roof as they rolled. Then, they were punching at each other in a flurry of dust, trying to land a hit, legs wrapped around torsos, gravity swerving up and down as they flipped each other. She landed a good punch in his stomach that took all the wind out of him, she grunted as she took one to the thigh, she was biting his shoulder, his neck. The pain that sprung up all over them kicked their adrenaline; Will moaned, Rhona panted.

Rhona straddled him, her hands at Will's throat, teeth gritted. Her ragged fingernails dug into his neck.

Will tried to scream, but he couldn't make a sound. He tried to tear her hands away, but she was far too strong. He felt his face, then his throat, then his lungs burn as he bucked his hips, trying to free himself. Everything swum through the air.

Then, a hot tear splashed on his cheek. Then another. The hands around his neck released.

Will's breath came out in rasps. Rhona wiped away her tears with the back of her hand; a violent, jerking motion.

When Will spoke, his voice sounded a lot like Rhona's. "It's okay. You win."

They panted for a while.

"Fine!" Rhona spat. "I'm the containment incident."

"What?"

"I was insubordinate. They took me into the labs. Then, they murdered me," Rhona snarled. She stood up. "They cut out my heart and programmed it back in," she jabbed her fingers into her temples, spit flying, "cut out bits of my brain and replaced them with wires and clockwork!"

She stood back. "I'm an inhuman *thing*. Out here with all these other things that aren't animal or human or machine. I don't even have a heartbeat." Her mismatched eyes shone in the light, and grimy tears cut through the dirt on her skin.

Will backed away.

"I see that look on your face! I'm a mistake they couldn't kill, a weapon that's useless because it feels. They rebuilt my hands out of metal? All the better to crush their throats!" Rhona fiercely wiped away her tears again.

Will shook his head. "No."

"Yeah! Fine! Scream, run! Like anybody should. I don't care."

Will took a deep breath and moved closer.

"Shoot me! Finally wipe the abomination that I am off this earth that I plague, day after day! Because not a day goes by that I'm not haunted by them. I don't even know which parts of me are natural—" Will gently took her hands "—and which are mechanical!" Rhona trailed off in surprise, staring at Will's hands in hers. She let go, and opened her arms.

Will yanked Rhona forward and kissed her. Her mouth was warm, wet; his cheeks flared up with heat. Then, he pushed her away, staring in shock.

"You're the one who did that, not me," Rhona mumbled.

They were silent for a minute.

"Alright. I understand why you don't trust me," Will said, rubbing his bruised neck, cheeks still burning. "But you're more than that. A containment incident, I mean. So please, don't . . . call yourself an abomination. You're the single most captivating human being I've ever met."

Rhona smiled; one of disbelief that slowly melted into believing.

"You know I wouldn't have survived out here without you," Will said, talking vaguely to the floor.

"Literally, not even a minute," Rhona chuckled softly.

He looked back up again. "Yeah, not even a minute. So . . . thank you."

"You still leaving?" Then she scoffed. "Yeah. You should go. Why would you stay out here in a deadly radioactive wasteland? Don't be silly," she said, more to herself. "Go. Before I put you in the stew."

"I don't want to abandon you, like the rest of humanity."

Rhona chuckled. "Nonsense."

Will raised an eyebrow. "I would try my best to—well—protect you, if you came with me, not that you can't look after yourself . . ."

"With a rusty saw?" She gave him a gentle slap on the leg. "Go on, you idiot. Fates smile upon you. Catch you later, if you fall through a rubbish chute, or something."

Will nodded, made himself smile.

At least you kissed her goodbye.

"Goodbye, Rhona. I understand why you don't want to . . . but I want to go home." Will walked beyond the firelight into the gloom.

Darkness, then light.

Will stood back in the evacuation portal centre. He sighed and walked away.

Behind him, her voice said, "You win."

About the Author:

Emily Siggs is a writer, editor and poet with a propensity for the delightfully bizarre. You can fine one of her other short stories, 'The Bindi', in the Cancer anthology. She won the youth section of the 2016 Patron's Prize for Poets with 'Tuesday Mornings', and in 2020, conducted a project for the Centre for Stories on dancers from many cultures, Australian Aishwaryas. She is currently working on an experimental dark fantasy novella, 'Nefelibata'. Her Instagram handle is emilyexploresspace.

LIONESS

Nikky Lee

You found me on the plains sleeping with my cubs. A shot from your weapon sent us scattering into the bush, but not before one of your iron balls lodged in my chest. I remember the pain, the searing burn that curled through my ribs as the pride ran, as fast and far as we were able.

But it wasn't fast or far enough.

You followed. Tracked us down through the noon when the heat is worst. When we had to stop to let the little ones rest.

Aya sunk down beside me, licked the wound your iron left. "How is it?"

"It hurts, a bad hurt," I said, whimpering as the wound flared afresh.

When dark came and it was time to hunt, I couldn't move. My body was heavy, my legs weak, claws and teeth blunt with fatigue.

When my cubs came to suckle, they bumped the wound and I snarled at them to stay away.

Nussa nudged them back with her nose. "Be off Seyha, Senga. Let your mother rest."

The next morning my world was dim and I couldn't lift my head.

"Nurse them," I begged Nussa. Her cubs were older, but she still produced milk.

"Do not fear," she said. "They will not go hungry." She dropped down beside me, the warmth of her body seeping into my cooling one. "I will take care of them."

"I don't want to go."

Aya nestled in too. "Rest. Go with the Earth."

But I did not rest. Because you found me. We heard you coming in your cars. They rumble like rain season thunder. Impossible not to hear when we're alert. We were that time, not like the first. Your weapons and shouting did the rest. My family broke for the horizon, vanishing into the haze with nothing but paw prints in their wake. I yearned to follow, to hunt the nights away with my mother, aunts and sisters; to play with my cubs. But my body ached, the pain deep, blood oozing. So, when you pointed the barrel at my head, I was ready. Soon it would be over.

But I did not go to the Earth. I stayed.

I watched you pose with my body. You splayed me out on my belly, put your boots on my back as if I were a mountain you'd conquered, not the mother you'd caught unawares as she rested from feeding her family.

Death is the way of things, I consoled myself. My meat will feed another family. Another mother, another cub. They will grow strong. My strength will become theirs, just as my prey had strengthened me.

But you took my body away, far away, and paid a man to remove my skin. He dumped my meat and bones in the dirt and left them there, a free meal for the vultures. You thanked him, rolled me up like an armadillo and stuffed me in a suitcase.

This is the end of it, I thought. I can go. Earth take me.

But then came the sounds. Rumbling engines, whining turbines—I have names for these now, I have done a lot of watching while you've been away. You took me to your homeland on the other side of the world, far from my beloved grasslands. And when light returned, you rolled me open; unfurled me on your floor. And there I've stayed. Waiting, watching, longing for the earth of my home.

There are no antelope here, no wildebeest migration to follow. Just an old cat who hisses at my skin when he's allowed into your study. There are books though. I read them over your shoulder— that took some seasons to learn. But when you read aloud to your cub, it made it easier to grasp. He's quite the sweetheart, isn't he? All blue-eyed and chubby. What's the phrase you people use? Could eat him right up? Yes, a gorgeous cub.

But shh, hush now, stop struggling, let me finish.

I learned many things in your room; I might have been happy to stay there. To watch and haunt that space. Until you did *that*. A holiday, I thought. You've had a few over the years. But this one was longer. Not your weekend getaway to the Hamptons. It doesn't take a baboon to work out you'd gone abroad.

Day in day out, I paced, my spirit rustling papers on your desk. I've been getting good at that, you know? That chill your wife complains of in the lounge? That's me prowling past. The creaking floorboards that wake your son at night? I'm there in his room.

Then you returned. You opened your suitcase and I saw a new skin. Tan fur, rounded ears, lips pulled back into a snarl. You spread it out beside mine. Golden fur; mouth forever frozen in a snarl. A lioness killed in her prime.

And I knew rage.

I know my kin anywhere. My cub. My baby. My Sehya. Gone to the Earth too soon.

"Murderer!" I snarled, and the walls shivered. You felt it, oh yes, I saw how you jumped. You called out to your wife: "Did you feel that?"

She put your fears to rest. "Feel what?"

And like that, you shrugged and dismissed it.

Dismissed me.

You should not have done that.

Quiet now, it'll all be over soon.

LIONESS

You were tired from your trip, see? Thought to do some work before dinner, but exhaustion got the better of you. I sang you a lullaby I once sang to my cub now lying there on the floor. Your eyelids drooped; you rested your head on your desk. And I took my chance.

I pounced. My skin wrapping you tight, muffling your scream. We fell to the floor you and I, a tangle of skin and fur. My teeth found your throat and I *squeezed*.

And now here we are.

You writhe, but I writhe with you, learning how you move; how all those bones and muscles work together. My skin sticks to your back, curls around your belly, pulls over your face. There's a crunch of bones breaking and remaking. Our vision darkens. Our body drops to all fours.

Your screams fade.

Hush now. This lion is done sleeping.

About the Author:

Nikky grew up as a barefoot 90s child in Perth, Western Australia, before moving to New Zealand in 2016. By day she works as a professional content writer and by night authors speculative fiction, often burning the candle at both ends to explore fantastic worlds, mine asteroids and meet wizards. Her creative work has appeared in magazines, on radio and in anthologies around the world. She is currently writing a dark fantasy trilogy, routinely sacrificing literary darlings to the editing gods in the hopes of seeing it published.

You can find her online at:
W:nikkythewriter.com | T:@NikkyMLee | F:nikkythewriter

THE GOLDEN LION-MONKEY

Alannah K. Pearson

Leontopithecus aureus minor (Leo, 1886)

I hereby describe a new species of small primate,
Leontopithecus aureus minor or the Small Golden Lion-Monkey,
discovered during the recent expeditions in the jungles of The
Twin Majesties' Brazilian colonies. The explorations and
subsequent scientific expeditions of the coastal lowlands
surrounding the Brazilian colonies have revealed many new and
fascinating fae creatures not known within the lands of the British
Isles or elsewhere within The Twin Majesties' Empire. Among
these fascinating discoveries have been the spectacular *Draconem
ignis oculare*, a diminutive morph native to Brazil, whose gaze is
capable of incinerating entire buildings. Although the initial
descriptions suggested that the Small Golden Lion-Monkey might
be an undiscovered fae race of diminutive arboreal lion, I hereby

provide evidence to the contrary. The Golden Lion-Monkey is, in fact, unrelated to any of the fae races yet discovered. The discovery of this new species by Leo in the year 1886 represents one of the most spectacular small primates from the distant jungles of the New Worlds.

"The year of my birth, many mediums and fortune-tellers were convinced great change was coming. My mother believed in the astrological signs which were *in vogue* that year, and to please her, my father proclaimed when his son was born, he would name him Leo for the famed courage of the lion. Of course, I was born a girl-child, not the son my father had hoped for, nor was I gifted the name he had reserved."

"But you are still Leo, my lady."

I glanced to my maidservant's refection in the looking glass.

"Tomorrow is my eighteenth birthday, Delia," I continued as she bustled around behind me. "My father never had a male heir, so this estate will be my future husband's property. How is that just?"

Delia smiled with understanding and tucked a wayward red curl behind her stern white servant's kerchief, then held up the black lacquered box of jade hair pins, presenting them to me as if they were a priceless treasure.

I sighed. Considering the man who had bestowed this gift on me, they probably were.

"There is no justice in this world, my lady," Delia agreed. "But perhaps this exquisite gift from Lord James Amsworth might make some amends for society's broader failings?"

"Am I supposed to swoon with appreciation?" I asked, rolling my eyes.

"I'm told all the ladies do," she said, placing the lacquered box with reverence on the dresser.

I peered suspiciously at it as though it might attack. "Why me?"

"I would say it was your sparkling wit," she said. "But you'd not believe me."

"No." I paused, hearing the scuff of shoes outside my bedchamber. "I am like pedigree livestock to him," I said, a conspiratorial smile at Delia. "Do you think he'd ever believe me a bastard?"

A shocked gasp from the beyond my bedchamber doorway, confirmed my suspicion that the older housemaid was eavesdropping.

"Let's get on with it then," I said, gesturing to Delia to open the box.

She moved forward with determination, beginning the artful arrangement of my hair that would be a centrepiece for today. Delia gossiped while she worked, deft fingers twisting and plaiting my hair into meticulous braids, my dark curls decorated with the pale jade pins.

I twirled a hairpin between my fingertips, inspecting its tiny sculpted flowers and quality craftsmanship while Delia finished the braiding. I glowered at my own reflection as Delia snatched the last pin, securing my hair in place.

"What do you think a gift of hair pins really means, Delia?" I asked as she prepared my elaborate dress, heavy with embroidery.

"I believe it means he thought to impress you, my lady."

"Hm," I said, stepping into the dress, bracing myself as she began to tighten the corset ties. "Are you sure it doesn't mean he is hoping our marriage will provide wealth to secure his future business endeavours? Or do you think hairpins suggest I have failed to accessorise fashionably enough?"

"I don't think he noticed your hair, my lady," Delia chuckled.

"Really?" I asked. "He spends a great deal of his own fortune on exotic perfumes for himself and diamonds for his earlobes. I would expect he'd want a wife he could dress meticulously to match his attire to bring out when necessary?"

"That seems a very harsh criticism."

"Possibly," I sighed. "I have no interest in this gallery opening this morning, Delia. I had heard among the members of the Zoological Society that James Amsworth had a passion for the discoveries of the New Worlds."

"Then perhaps instead of Rosanna Corrano attending a gallery opening, Doctor Leo should invite James Amsworth for an evening of carousing?"

"I do not think James Amsworth prefers the company of men."

Delia suppressed a laugh, coughing quietly into her elbow. "Let's tighten the rest of this torture instrument."

I braced myself against the pain from my healing ribs as Delia tightened and secured the corset, the dull ache a remnant of an injury earned as my alternate persona.

I had spoken true my assessments of James Amsworth, noted when assuming my socially appropriate role as Lady Rosanna Corrano, and also when associating with James Amsworth as Doctor Leo, a London scientist who not only did not exist but was the only woman to have infiltrated the male-dominated world of the natural sciences. If I could, I would have lived every day as Leo, but he had no real place in the London society ruled by The Twin Majesties, where Victor and Victoria decided the law and ideals of the Empire.

As it was inappropriate in Victorian society for an unmarried young woman such as myself to travel anywhere unaccompanied, Delia stood with me under the protection of the portico while we waited for the carriage. I stared at the drizzling rain. The driveway to my father's estate was a sweeping circular affair, the front gates hidden from our view by a small woodland. It was a pretence of the idyllic countryside, the stretch of lawn between the manor and that copse of trees was all that stood between us the rest of the London city.

Footmen hurried to help Delia and I into the carriage and with strict instructions from my father's manservant, we were soon rattling along the broad avenue of stately houses and small city estates just like our own. These grand boulevards stretched like four spokes on a carriage wheel to intersect with the towering form of the royal castle which loomed above the city centre like a spectre.

The view of the city beyond the carriage window was obscured by mist or pollution and, clutching at my parasol, I considered how I was about to be paraded through the gallery as if I were an item on show like the paintings. This event felt like a charade contrived so London society might see Lord James Amsworth and Lady Rosanna Corrano in each other's company and intense speculation could begin about our prospects. The helplessness of my situation made me grind my teeth in frustration.

"My lady?"

I met Delia's concerned gaze. A few rebellious red curls had escaped their bondage again, threatening to incite more.

"Delia," I said, smoothing the edges of my fingerless lace gloves. "How do you manage to control my hair so skilfully when your own looks like a viper's nest?"

"Some parts of us are easier controlled than others, my lady."

"Well said." I smiled. "You remind me that though I wear the accoutrements of a noble woman today, my spirit will always be that of Leo."

"Maybe one day you can be whole, my lady," she said, glancing at me. "There are many areas of this city where one such as yourself could live openly."

"Disreputable areas?" I asked, quirking an eyebrow.

"Maybe," she said with a grin. "But ones where life has more freedom."

"Albeit also shorter," I sighed. "No, Delia. I am as much Rosanna as I am Leo. Perhaps you could run some errands today for Doctor Leo?"

"And leave you and Lord Amsworth unaccompanied? Such a thing is scandalous, and I would likely lose my position for it, my lady."

"Lord Amsworth assures me his elderly aunt is accompanying us." I squeezed her hand. "This horrid gallery is her idea apparently."

"You believe him?" Delia asked, raising her eyebrows.

"Unfortunately, yes," I sighed as the carriage pulled sharply to a halt before the museum steps. "I imagine he is as thoughtless as everything has previously indicated."

Delia frowned. "Are you certain you don't judge him unfairly? Perhaps even against rationality, my lady?"

I ignored her accusation as the mech-work iron steps rolled into place.

The footmen opened the door and, placing my embroidered slipper on a step, held my hand out to the footman for assistance. Once on the footpath, I turned to Delia as she climbed more easily from the carriage, the simple servant's attire less cumbersome.

"What could be better to inspire a woman's fragile mind than an entire gallery of still-life paintings?" I asked.

Delia grimaced. "My errands suddenly sound much more appealing," she waved the note I had given her in the air. "You need these collected for the auction Doctor Leo is attending tonight?"

Scanning the crowd gathered on the wide front steps of the building, I nodded in agreement to Delia, watching her quick bow of acknowledgment before she joined the flow of servants and merchants on their daily errands.

I turned to the wide front steps of the building behind me, the classical-stylise colonnades replicating Greco-Roman architecture. Staring up at the leaden grey sky and the soot-covered stonework, I longed to disappear into the crowd and follow Delia.

"Lady Corrano." The familiar soft tenor made my heart drop.

Nodding to my footmen and turning, I smiled to Lord Amsworth as he approached, engraved walking cane clicking in time with his boots. My smile faltered as his gaze swept appreciatively over my form, inspecting me like I was an object to be admired.

"You are alone?" he asked, frowning. "No concern. My aunt insisted she attend today's gallery event," he continued to smile benignly but sounded less than pleased.

"My thanks," I acknowledged. "I asked my maidservant to attend to important errands while we attend the gallery. I can't imagine she would find such things of interest."

He smiled but a small frown creased his brow. "Let me escort you inside. The weather is near a tempest out here."

"My thanks," I mumbled again, squinting at the fine drizzle falling from the sky.

Lord Amsworth formally bowed to me, offering his arm.

I placed my own atop his, our gloved hands touching. I lifted my free hand self-consciously to my hair, checking the complex plaiting of my hair was intact.

"I see you're wearing the jade," he commented, smiling as he helped me climb the stairs. "It looks as pleasing as I'd hoped."

"Forgive me." I blushed, thinking what a vain fool he must think me. "I'd not sent proper word yet to thank you for such a magnificent gift."

He waved away my comment but there was a self-satisfied edge to his smile. It annoyed me that he thought my affections I could be bought by expensive trinkets and praises. He was pleased with his efforts, seeming to preen like a peacock as we stepped into the large atrium to the Natural History Museum. A poor choice of husband he would make, I thought, observing him from beneath my lashes.

The spacious atrium was met by an arching stairway leading to the upper balconies where many of the exhibits were often held. Without thinking, I continued toward the stairwell. A gentle but firm pressure on my elbow guided me back toward the centre of the space, a curious but still pleasant smile quirking Lord Amsworth's lips as he steered me toward the hallway to the far left.

I returned the questioning lift of his brows with a quick, apologetic smile and cast my eyes to the floor. That had been foolish. Except for very rare public events, the upper balconies were never open to women. No wonder he kept giving me curious glances. I did not speak as we made our way through the public hallways of the lower level, smiling genially to acquaintances as we progressed toward the large room opening into a conservatory at the rear of the building.

The spacious gallery at the end of the hallway was adorned with canvases depicting various still-life arrangements. On days like today when the London sky was a leaden, soot-stained grey, this room was often so dimly lit as to be impassable. Today, the space was so well illuminated it rivalled only the large museum atrium for brightness. I quickened my step toward what appeared to be a large glass sphere in the centre of the gallery, clusters of people taking tea and macaroons from the lavishly supplied tables. How had they achieved such illumination? This was more than simple gas lamps or chandeliers could provide. What marvel was this?

James Amsworth gave me another curious little smile as I nearly dragged him toward the bright orb hanging from the ceiling beams. Light poured into every nook and corner of the gallery, banishing even the thinnest shadows. As I drew closer, I saw the tiny glittering forms dancing within the glass sphere, their lithe bodies just visible from the brilliance they emitted.

"Pixies," I breathed, staring in fascination.

Amsworth peered at the glass. "I had heard about these."

"You've never seen pixies?" I asked, confused.

"Of course, I've seen pixies. Every child has chased pixies at twilight," he said, chuckling at my confusion. "No, I refer to hearing about this proposal to the City Council to install spheres such as these as a safer alternative to gas lamps."

I frowned. "Using pixies as a source for public lighting?"

"Yes," he said, nodding approvingly. "An ingenious proposal. Just imagine the savings to the public purse if gas lighters were not required anymore, the countless fires and deaths avoided. Not to mention, that noxious smell."

I considered his argument while watching the many bright shifting bodies within the glass. To illuminate a room this size there must have been nearly a hundred of the fae within the massive glass bulb. I shuddered to think how a growing city the size of London proposed to provide a continuous supply of pixies.

"Do the pixies always remain within the glass?"

"I think it's much like an aquarium or aviary," he said, surveying the room for his aunt.

"Have you heard of other similar endeavours?"

"Hm?" he asked, gesturing above my head for a servant to attend us.

I gently touched his arm, receiving his undivided attention. "Are there other things where the fae are used in such a way?"

"You're really interested in the fae?" he asked, frowning.

"Yes," I said, accepting a fine teacup and pink macaroon from the servant.

"Oh," he considered for a moment, sipping his tea. "Well, I know it is quite common now to use selkies in the shipping industry."

"Selkies?" I blurted, trying not to spill my tea in surprise.

"They're like mermaids but able to transform into seals," he answered, frown deepening.

"Oh." I gulped my tea, cursing myself for not feigning nonchalance. "How can selkies be useful in shipping?"

"I have used them myself when shipping goods through dangerous waters. The selkies guide the ships around shoals, reefs, through sudden storms and into safe harbours. It has saved a great deal of cargo and lives from shipwreck."

"It seems very good of the selkies to help us in such endeavours," I said, keeping my eyes downcast to hide how unlikely I thought that occurring without considerable coercion.

"I later discovered they don't do it for love of humanity," he confided. "They live in clans and are loyal to only one queen. Each harbourmaster has stolen a pelt from a selkie queen and so she and her clan are beholden to whoever has her pelt. That is the only reason they help us."

"Oh," I breathed. I stared at the macaroon; the bite of sugary pastry suddenly felt dry in my mouth. How long has such scientific endeavours as these been going on without my notice? How many of my fellow scientists were abusing the fae in such ways?

James Amsworth covertly watched me while I forced myself to eat the macaroon and drink the tea. I often felt his eyes upon me, noticed his frown deepening. It seemed very likely I need not worry about having to marry him. He had probably already decided I was an unsuitable match.

The morning continued with unsurpassed tedium. Amsworth followed his aunt, hand on my elbow as we progressed around the gallery. I could not disguise my disinterest in still-life paintings and the sight of another sunflower on a kitchen table drove me to despair. I begged to be excused and, without waiting for Amsworth's response, I rushed from the gallery. I heard only a snippet of a whispered disapproval from his aunt as I escaped into the atrium beyond.

In the cool expanse of the museum atrium, I paced before the front steps, trying to calm my outrage. I kept recalling the shimmering faces of the pixies trapped within the glass and could not escape the thoughts that I was not dissimilar from a bird within a cage, a pixie within a glass prison.

"Lady Corrano?" Amsworth called from behind me.

I paused, already pulling on my leather gloves to protect against the chill outside. I turned to face him. "Forgive my departure, I'm suddenly very weary."

"Of course," he replied, already gesturing to one of the waiting footmen near the main door. "But I apologise if this morning was not to your liking."

"I am not well-suited to still-life paintings," I admitted.

"Nor am I," he said and bowed to take his leave. As he straightened, he offered me a museum pamphlet.

I frowned and, taking the public announcement, turned it over to read the text. It concerned the newest discoveries in the natural sciences made during recent expeditions to the New Worlds.

"I know some gentlemen might think it endearing that ladies could find such scientific matters interesting, but it's only to be expected. Perhaps you might like to accompany me to the exhibition on this fae creature, the Golden Lion-Monkey?"

I read several of the purported discoveries from the Brazilian jungles, including a golden fae lion that lived in the trees like monkeys but was smaller than a kitten. "I would be honoured to accompany you."

Amsworth smiled and gave a mock-exaggerated bow. He straightened nodded toward my attendants who waited on the main steps, carriage driver already opening the door. I watched Amsworth walk away, disappearing among the crowd. Still confused by the events of the morning, I turned to the waiting carriage, rain already falling in heavy drops.

"Well?" Delia called before the carriage door was even closed.

"Still-life paintings are perfectly horrendous," I replied, settling into the seat as the carriage began to move.

"I meant Lord Amsworth, my lady."

"He did not seem that impressed with the paintings either."

"I don't imagine many gentlemen are," she chuckled. "Was he impressed with you?"

"Until a moment ago I would have sworn he was like any other gentleman I've ever had the misfortune to spend a dinner party seated beside. But then he seemed to speak more openly. Perhaps it was only to flatter me, but it seems unlikely to applaud my interest in science for the sake of flattery. He asked me to accompany him to the exhibition on the natural science discoveries from Brazil."

Delia clapped her hands like a child. "That's marvellous."

"Perhaps," I agreed then frowned, considering my more immediate issues. "Before you wish me luck in my future happiness, did you complete those errands?"

"For Doctor. Leo, you mean?" she teased. "And I've made the usual arrangements so you can depart directly after supper."

"I can't miss tonight's auction," I muttered, hand to my side as the carriage jolted me, corset painfully compressing my bruised ribs. "I can't wait to be free of this thing."

Later that evening, I hastened through the dim illumination of the gas lamps positioned along the city streets. the Natural History

Museum. London at night was a very different world from the one I had walked in only several hours earlier. Time and space seemed disconnected at night, the dense fog warping perception, echoes from those selling wares along the docks and gardens seemed impossibly close. Turning aside from the London streets, the Natural History Museum loomed in front of me, appearing from the veil of shifting shadow and river mist. My bootheels clicked on the stone steps, walking cane swinging idly in one hand as I took the stairs several at a time.

As Rosanna, I was not unknown in these parts of London but the metamorphosis I had undergone for this return visit, as with many of my others, ensured that no one would recognise me from earlier that day. Now dressed in a gentleman's finely tailored trousers; a crisp white shirt Delia had acquired earlier under the name of Doctor Leo. Tonight, was not my first venture into London society in the guise of my alternate persona but it was one of the more formal events held under the auspicious London Society of the Natural Sciences. Still unaccustomed with the more elaborate attire, I fidgeted with the stiff embroidered waistcoat which was uncomfortably tight where the bindings around my chest hid any evidence of my more feminine attributes.

Once inside the atrium of the Museum, I followed several other scientists I recognised in the procession up the sweeping staircase to the upper level balconies and private rooms. Pausing on the landing for a moment to catch my breath, I checked the correct time using the large bronze timepiece in the atrium.

Removing my fob watch, I checked the synchronicity of the timepieces before rallying my courage and hastened up the remaining stairs. There were only a few moments to spare before proceedings would get underway.

At the end of a narrow hall, double doors opened into a lavishly proportioned room. Pausing on the threshold, I noticed the room was well illuminated with smaller versions of the pixie lamps. Entering slowly, I wondered which of my scientist colleagues at this auction had conceived such an abhorrent idea.

"Doctor Leo," a junior society member announced well-after I'd entered, giving me an apologetic smile.

I nodded to the young man but continued toward the table bowing beneath the weight of goblets and wine bottles. Reaching for a decanter, my hand was enveloped in a familiar firm handshake and an older man pulled me toward a quiet corner.

"Forgive the boy on the door," he said, passing me a glass of sherry. "He's been excited to meet you all week."

"A student of yours, Professor?" I asked, taking a small sip.

"A bright young man but still much too impressionable."

"I recall being just as young and enthusiastic once," I said wistfully.

Of course, I had never been who any of these distinguished professors and scientists thought me to be. Most of these learned men would be outraged to know their exclusive society had been infiltrated by a woman; let alone those members who had conducted research alongside me.

The professor raised his glass in salute. "To youth," he offered.

It seemed a very good thing to honour and so I drank from my sherry and listened to the conversations and debates around us. Men who could be the most rational of scientists but opposed to each other's interpretations of describing fae races began a vocal debate in the centre of the room.

Abruptly, the auctioneer called for silence. I smiled in knowing appreciation and moved to my seat nearer the raised dais at the front of the room. There was a long catalogue listing the new discoveries from various expeditions throughout Their Twin Majesties' colonies. While many of the discoveries were fascinating, I was most interested in the later section of the catalogue. Toward the back of the catalogue, auction items were listed from expeditions to the Brazilian colonies of the New Worlds.

Ever since Lord Amsworth had drawn my attention, I had become increasingly fascinated throughout the afternoon by the so-called fae species, the Golden Lion-Monkey as it was called. The final item on tonight's auction offered the opportunity to study the new fae creature caught from the wild Brazilian jungle and publish the discovery. It was to any scientist's greatest honour to study and name a species, especially one as intriguing as this new fae creature promised.

The evening drew late and still many scientists were in the room, talking and occasionally making bids for their colleges or museums on various items. A moderately-sized wrought-iron cage was wheeled into the centre of the room. I sat up straighter, staring at the thick embroidered cloth which covered the cage. The material was embossed with the distinctive emblem for the Natural History Museum. The young boy who had been announcing the arrivals earlier in the evening stood poised behind the cage. He gave an expert flourish and drew away the cloth.

Along with every other scientist in the room, I let out an audible exclamation of astonishment. The sound of hushed conjecture began from the scientists seated around the room but I scarcely heard the auctioneer call for silence. Instead, I leaned toward the cage, chin on my hands, staring in wonder at the tiny monkey in the cage. The pamphlet had been correct, it *was* no larger than a domestic kitten and it climbed the branches arranged in its cage as naturally as any monkey. But as I looked from the brilliant gold of the mane around its shoulders, the tufted tail and claws on its tiny hands and feet, I knew this creature was no more any kind of fae lion than I was. The small face turned to the audience and the little monkey barred its long canine teeth. It was not a fae creature but somehow more wondrous for it.

When the auctioneer called for bidding, I quickly raised my hand.

It was several months later, when Lord Amsworth and Rosanna were expected to attend the latest premiere exhibition at the Natural History Museum. Although, we had been seen at a few minor public events together and, despite a deepening of my trust in his character, I still did not want to marry and be forced to relinquish what freedoms the life of Doctor Leo provided me. In many respects, my existence as Rosanna had become more a shadow-life than the supposed falsehood of my pseudonym.

Outside the museum, Lord Amsworth bowed as was proper for a gentleman meeting a young woman in public. Straightening, he offered his arm. I assessed the more confined bodice and skirt of my new dress; I gratefully took his elbow.

I balanced my weight against him as we climbed the stone staircase. The latest fashion of the London dressmakers made such tasks near impossible without assistance. Pausing briefly in the atrium to re-arrange the embroidered hem of the dress, we began the slow ascent up the marble staircase to the upper levels of the museum where public exhibitions were rarely conducted. While I fondly recalled the ease of such climbs in trousers, the disparity of the freedoms offered to me as Leo but denied to Rosanna weighed heavier upon me each day.

"You seem pensive today," James Amsworth commented.

"I was contemplating the future."

We reached the upper level where gold roped sections directed us toward a large exhibition area at the far end of the balcony.

"The future must be bleak to make you so sad."

I stopped moving, turning to face him. "Perhaps it is only bleak if I allow it."

"That seems a very logical conclusion," he agreed as we began walking again.

"Do you know much about the Brazilian colonies?" I asked.

"No," he laughed. "I was very much hoping you might explain it to me."

I frowned at the strangeness of his reply. It was incredibly unlikely that any woman or man in London society would have much knowledge about the Brazilian expeditions in the New Worlds. Why then would he imagine Rosanna could explain it? Surely, he did not allude to what I thought he did? There was no foreseeable way he could know about my alternate persona as Doctor Leo.

"I will try," I finally answered, sounding doubtful.

The second floor of the museum was divided into various prominent exhibits from the New Worlds. A large crowd of London's society members were mingling at the far end, the fluttering of women's large feather fans was like a dizzying flock of strange jewel-coloured birds. James' hand on my elbow was a comfort as we negotiated the crowd of people to reach the first of the raised platforms displaying various botanical discoveries. Without comment, James plucked a pamphlet from somewhere behind me, offering it to me. I stared uncomprehending for a moment, eyes refusing to focus on the printed words as sudden anxiety rose in me.

"Do you know Doctor Leo?" James asked, crossing his arms.

Forcing myself to breathe slowly, calmly my erratic pulse, I dared another glance at the familiar words I had penned only weeks ago. Or rather, Doctor Leo had penned. Why was James asking about whether I knew a London scientist? I forced myself to look properly at the grainy photograph that accompanied a description of the golden lion-monkey. Squinting at the image of a young man holding his arm outstretched, the golden lion-monkey climbing with ease toward his slender wrist.

"I have heard Doctor Leo is an eminent scientist," I said, peering at James. "Why do you ask?"

"I thought he might be a relative," he said. "There seemed some resemblance to you."

My heart faltered in my chest. The room seemed suddenly too crowded, the flutter of fans and sound of pages turning in paper pamphlets was impossibly loud. I glanced about nervously, feeling the slight perspiration on my skin. I glanced up at James who remained motionless, face forced in a blank expression. Waiting. He was waiting for me to respond. Did he know? How could he know? If I admitted my deception, the freedoms I enjoyed could be stripped away forever. My existence as Doctor Leo was the nourishment my mind and spirit needed. How could I explain that to James? How could I explain that Rosanna could only endure the confines of her daily prison for freedoms Doctor Leo was allowed.

"Rosanna," James said. "You know I care deeply for you. I hoped we might enjoy each other's trust so that one day, you might consider doing me the honour of becoming my wife. But I can see you do not trust easily. I planned today to offer you something as a sign of my trust and faith in you. I hope you might feel you can respond in kind, and return some trust in me. You are also aware I own one of the prominent London printing presses. I want to offer you the chance to publish this scientific discovery."

I remained silent, staring at James as my mind struggled to accept the gravity of what he was offering me. What he understood of me. Was James truly admitting to not just knowing that Rosanna Corrano and Doctor Leo were one in the same, albeit split between two very different versions of the same person, was he admitting such a thing did not offend or disgust him? I could hardly grasp the gravity of what such a revelation might mean for me. It seemed too much to hope that James could love me, truly for who *I* was, to see beyond the outward appearances of Rosanna or Leo.

James swore quietly under his breath and blushed apologetically. "Rosanna," he began, taking my gloved hands. "I know Doctor Leo will be unable to attend any public events if you are present. I *know*."

The strength of what James conveyed in that single word took my breath from my lungs. He clearly did not want to force any confrontation from me, and trust was something I could give him, but he could never take from me. This awkward conversation was an elegant way of showing me the truth of his conviction. There was great humility in that, and it broke every wall I had constructed to prevent myself from trusting him, seeing who he had always been.

"How long have you known?" I asked, small smile lifting the corners of my mouth.

Relief relaxed the tension around his lips, and he returned my smile. "I greatly suspected since the still-life paintings."

Looping my arm through his, I glanced back toward the exhibition. "Since Doctor Leo cannot be in attendance today, let me show you *my* work."

About the Author:

Alannah K. Pearson is a speculative fiction author, combining her interests and expertise in archaeology and ancient history, global folktales, mythologies and environment. Alannah's writing interests include Amerindian folktales, Norse mythology, Prehistory, Archaeology, Ancient History and Gothic folklore. Alannah also has an academic background in Archaeology, Prehistory and human evolution. When not writing, Alannah is completing a PhD in human and primate evolution or enjoying the Australian wilderness with two dogs (canine assistants). She is a keen nature and wildlife photographer, bookshop and Museum devotee.
Alannah K. Pearson lives in Canberra, Australia. You can follow her at www.alannahkpearson.com and @AlannahKPearson.

Hibernating Through The Apocalypse

Brianna Bullen

He'd killed a human, inhuman & strong

jaws clamped over artery, but not as a tourniquet.

He needed to wait out suspicion

away from tracker dog fellows &

hunters eager to enact blood vengeance

upon an animal reacting

to territorial instinct.

Perhaps this was human territory, exceptionalism.

Snorting wet through snail-shell

nostrils, he engine-exhaust exhaled

& lumbered, woodsman and wolf both, jacked up

muscles tectonic moving under every motion.

His stalk-less mushroom ears twitched slowly,
sensing no stalkers nearby.
He finds a hideout. Shakes out his mane like
auburn autumn leaves.

Mocking the humans on two legs, he lazy-paws
the tree, bark as scratch post, whining in communion
with the tree
under his claws. Mutual pleasure groans.
And so, the lion becomes bear and hibernates from life,
curled up
deep inside the hollow of a secret,
an oak surrounded by lily-white daisies and paper plates.
The smallest drops
are confetti static, buoyed snow in the late autumn
breeze
white and oil-ashen as the winter time ushers in.
Such presents from safari
get scarcer in the off-season.
His oak -prison held strong, keeping him a safe
Shakespeare's Ariel, suspended
in timeless-time inside while centuries passed, eras
blinking
by in trails of lifetimes. Outside his corpse-cushioned
den—red rock rats survivalist stockpiles now open
ribbed stripped—

the tree had been bleached in bark and branch
the ghosts of leaves drifting by a memory of another
time and for another time. Green has turned into a
dream, the moss rotted to the grey of faded tea cosies.
Damp and dry air wheezes in competition, damp
winning out only
in the shadows. Trees are erect cigarettes, smoking
from all sides. The only sounds are his paws padding
and cracking
over ground branched with skeletons.
He needed to move, to see—there was no time
for yawning and mourning. Not until he could grasp the
well-depth
of loss. Nuclear smog
and the ground exhales, air hissing beware.
A forest should not be so vacant
from the chatter of living beings. Fish corpses
decay on the water's oily skin, burning gelatine stench
over solid slicks, shifting in industrial psychedelic
heaves.
Destruction so wholesale
it cannot even be described as wanton—
for what pleasure could be derived from this?
A world of colour now in tie-dye greys, tyre die stains
and depthless blacks—
that which is visible through the white-out fog.

Body rebooting robot creaking,

processing at Ent-speed the deaths of his friends. Eyes

peeping

Felidae amber, polished glossy as glass

reflecting a world bewitched by short-sightedness.

This world is archaic silence. All he has is a heartbeat

stutter. For this world, there are no words:

no human-words

no forest-words

no lying lion-words.

He slept through his old world's dying calls

So blissfully

he lived to be its powerless

witness. This new world

burns Phoenix-destruction and diesel fumes,

regeneration a residual adaptation.

If a lion dies

in the woods, and no one is around to see it,

does it truly die?

About the Author:

Brianna Bullen is a Deakin University PhD creative writing candidate writing about memory in science fiction. She has had work published in journals including LiNQ, Aurealis, Voiceworks, Rabbit, Multiverse: An anthology of international science fiction poetry, and Woolf Pack Zine.

She won the 2017 Apollo Bay short story competition and placed second in the 2017 Newcastle Short story competition. Her manuscript was previously a finalist in the 2018 Subbed In Poetry Chapbook competition. In 2018, she was part of Nexus, an Arts Access Victoria collective for artists with mental health recovery lived experience.

A CHANGELING OF ASLAN SIX

C.E. Rhoden

"This reading is very rare," said the meditech, a system-generated frown on its broad forehead. "I don't recall the last time I saw this gene marker. Not for several generations, that is certain."

Delu swallowed, her heart beating a frenzied rhythm. So soon after his birth, the news that her baby had some kind of genetic flaw sent a bone-deep quiver of terror through her exhausted body. She touched her forefinger to her son's head, where a patch of tawny hair lay flat against the curve of his skull. Several shades darker than her own, almost as dark as his father's, his brown skin was smooth and perfect.

He was perfect, every millimetre of him. How could there possibly be a problem?

From his seat beside her bed, her partner Areli leaned forward, his body tense and his hands clasped together.

"Nothing ever showed on any of our prenatal scans," he said. "What is this genetic marker? How could it have been missed?"

The meditech tilted its head to the side, placing the tip of one forefinger to its temple as it accessed a data set. Even as a child, Delu had never taken to the plastile features of the serving bots, and this one seemed worse than most, like a hologram with an ugly glitch. Its voice was heartbreakingly mild, system-attenuated to deliver bad news. "This marker is rare and is rarely tested for."

Delu let out a whimper. "Is it bad? How serious is our baby's condition, meditech?"

"It is life-changing."

Delu swapped agonised glances with Areli. By rights, he would be boarding Forrarder 589 the next day, having completed his duty to leave a healthy replacement on his home planet of Aslan Six. Delu herself was slated to take Forrarder 594 in five years' time, leaving their as-yet-unnamed son behind when she followed along Areli's spacetrail to the next habitable planet, the one to be terraformed by the team of Forrarder 589. There they would be reunited as partners, there they would work to terraform the future Aslan Seven into a home.

"Place the infant on the mat once more," said the meditech, bringing Delu's mind back to the present. "I will call Malonda back."

Delu didn't want to return the baby to the scanning mat. She was sure that only bad news would follow. The child would be deemed unviable, and their role to take their race further into space would be set back by years. Delu's heart contracted with pain as Areli leaned over her. She relaxed her grip as he lifted their son gently from her.

When Malonda the Senior Midwife came back into the birthing pod just a few moments later, Areli placed the baby onto the scanning pad, his movements stiff with reluctance.

Immediately the child began to cry with a volume that startled Delu, shocked them all. That bellow was much too loud to come from their son's tiny body. The baby swung his miniature fists with determination, as if he wanted to fight the entire planet at once.

Delu whimpered.

Areli placed a hand over his mouth to keep his own cry in check.

To Delu's surprise, the midwife looked at them with a smile, shaking her head of tight grey curls. "Do not despair," she advised. "Your child is rare, but his life will be good."

"Good?" repeated Delu. "How can you say so? The meditech says his condition is life-changing!"

"Meditechs by their nature do not always understand the significance of what they see. They are machines after all. Now, rest easy for a moment while I check your wonderful son."

"Wonderful!" said Areli near her ear. "Del, she says our boy is wonderful. What does she mean? I don't understand."

Delu made no answer, her eyes fixed intently on the midwife who repeated all the scans that the meditech had completed. It was confusing to see that Malonda worked with a smile on her face, as if the results appearing on the reader gave her great pleasure. The baby's bawling subsided as the midwife ran the scanning tool down each of his limbs, across his forehead, over his abdomen. If he had not been so new to the world—less than an hour old—Delu would have sworn that he was following every move the midwife made. His presence was like a new star, a new sun, marvellous and undeniable. *Surely there was nothing wrong with him!* The meditech got it wrong, Delu consoled herself. Surely.

After agonisingly long minutes, the midwife stood up, lifting the baby in her arms.

Delu leaned forward, expecting Malonda to hand the baby back to her, but instead she held him close, his face pressed to her shoulder while she patted his back.

"I hope you don't mind," she said, not even glancing at Delu or Areli. "We haven't been so blessed on Aslan Six for many generations."

"You speak of blessings, and of wonder," said Delu, choosing her words with care, "but the meditech indicated that our baby has some sort of birth defect."

"What!" Malonda turned around, surprised. She handed the child back with a small sigh of regret. "You misunderstood. This is no defect. This is our heritage. Your child is a shape-changer."

Delu looked at Areli, and he looked back at her, shrugging.

"Tell us, please," she said.

"One of the first Forrarders was a shape-changer. Don't they teach you youngsters any history?"

Delu shook her head, as did Areli beside her.

Malonda sighed. "Do you mind?" she asked, indicating a chair beside Areli's.

"Of course! Please sit down. Please, tell us."

Areli put his arm around Delu's shoulders, the baby held between them.

"Your baby is a shape-changer. A lion changeling, to be exact."

"A, a lie-on?" asked Areli.

Malonda lifted her hands into the air and flapped them. "Forrarding save us, has it been so long? They don't even teach you children about terran animals anymore?"

Delu nudged Areli with her elbow as he stiffened with outrage at being called a child. "Wait, Malonda," she said. "I know this word. There was a lion in our early reader screens—you must remember, Areli?" But her partner shrugged again. Delu went on. "It's an animal from old Terra. A great golden hunter, like a shipcat but much bigger. There must be images in the archives."

"That's right," said Malonda. "The first Forrarders left Terra after the big split. We don't have much information about what happened to Terra after that. What we do know is that five extended families set off to seek a new life on a new planet.

127

Generations passed before they found something they could inhabit."

"Oh," said Areli, echoing Delu's own thoughts. "You mean Aslan One. We learned about that. It was nearly right but they did some terraforming to improve it. That's how we started the terraformation teams."

"And then," added Delu, "before the planet of Aslan One could get overloaded with us humans and our needs, another set of Forrarders went out and found Aslan Two, didn't they?"

"You've got it," said Malonda. "Maybe history is still being taught. We Forrarders continued on and on till we are now at Aslan Six, leaving all the planets behind us with a small population stabilised by Forrarding." She grinned at them. "But let's get back to your marvel of a son."

"Please."

"One of the families had shape-changer abilities. It's not really a gene—it's more a kind of virus that gets expressed in some individuals. Hardly any of us carry the viral segments and very few of us have the right metabolism to allow the virus to flourish."

"Go on," said Areli.

At that moment, the baby launched into another ferocious howl of protest. Malonda rose and for a few minutes nothing more was said as she helped Delu settle the baby to her breast. When he was contentedly sucking, Delu looked up at the midwife.

"Tell us more. I'm terrified this baby isn't viable, and already I love him with all my heart. He's a shape-changer? He will grow into an animal from old Terra?"

"No! He will be strong and energetic and noisy. He will be wonderful with other children and he will make your home a precious place. He will eat a lot and talk a lot and grow red in the face with his energy. He will play hard and sleep hard and he will love you with all his heart. But sometimes he will transform into a lion, unpredictably."

Delu looked at Areli, and they both looked down at the contented child. "And this changes his life?"

"All your lives!" said Malonda. "Most Forrarder careers are closed to your son. Anything that involves pressurised safety gear is out. He can never board a forrarding ship, for one thing; he can never work outside the Dome. He is stuck on this planet, and inside this Dome, for the rest of his life."

There was a minute of silence as Delu and Areli looked down on the now sleeping infant. "Luan," said Delu. "Let's call him Luan. He's going to live all his life here on Aslan Six." She took a shaking breath. "Wherever we end up, he will never join us." A slow tear moved down her cheek. She could not imagine one day leaving this baby and never seeing him again.

"You two are not going anywhere!" said Malonda with a guffaw, astonishing them. She put one hand on Areli's shoulder and one on Delu's as she looked down on Luan with a smile. "You are all stuck here. Any plans for you to leave must be cancelled. You will continue your in-Dome assignments. Something in your genes allowed this to happen, and we Forrarders contain the shape-changer risk by keeping you here. That's why this is so rare—shape-changing is dangerous in space, and over the generations anybody with the potential has been kept planetside."

Delu looked at Areli. They had both learned their trades planetside and could easily deploy them planetside. They had simply always been brought up to believe that their destiny lay in taking the Forrarders forward. Now it seemed that they would become permanent residents, part of the small Dome community.

"You mean," said Delu, "that Areli and I can stay on Aslan Six our whole lives? Live our whole lives here, with our son?"

"That's exactly what I mean," said Malonda, getting to her feet. "Not such a bad thing, is it?"

Delu looked down at Luan, the weight of Areli's arm warm around her back. If Luan had not been so new to the world, she would have sworn that he was smiling.

She could have sworn that their baby was purring.

About the Author:

Clare Rhoden lives in Melbourne Australia with her husband and a highly intelligent poodle-cross called Aeryn.
Clare is an author, blogger and book reviewer inspired by politics, culture and history. Her novels include historical fiction 'The Stars in the Night' *and the dystopian trilogy* 'The Chronicles of the Pale.' *You can find Clare's books, blog posts and reviews at* https://clarerhoden.com.

THE HIDDEN BEAST

Kel E. Fox

Words circle overhead,

Waiting,

Ready to pick on my open mind

When I give up the battle.

And I will,

Because a shadow is frightening,

But a beast?

Not so much.

A beast I can fight

Or appeal to,

Defeat

Or fall down to,

In a flurry of claws and broken pride,

But no more would I wonder.

And so far

All I have had to do

Is stare it down,

Until I see it,

Until I know its name.

And when I do, the maned beast holds nothing,

A worthless hand.

Without a roar, it retreats,

But not into shadow.

Now, I see it sitting, away,

Forlorn,

Lost.

Wind fans the flaming mane,

Ruffles the tip of its tail.

After a time

I go to it,

Place a hand on its shoulder

Or flank

And offer it a word.

About the Author:

Kel E Fox ran an apothecary in a past life, was a stage technician before she finally embraced writing in this life and hopes to be a wizard in the next. She writes an eclectic mix of speculative fiction and is working on her debut release 'Darkhaven', *the first of a YA fantasy saga about a girl who gets struck by lightning, develops superpowers, stumbles into a global conspiracy and meets an alien god all in the same day.*

Kel lives in Perth, Australia with her life (and ballroom dancing) partner, two lazy cats and a wilful young Alaskan Malamute named after Nighteyes.

See more at <u>kelefox.com</u> *or find her on socials @kelelizabethfox*

EGYPTIAN PLAGUE

Phil Hore

<u>London, December 1968</u>

The bustle of a busy Wednesday morning in London is something to see. Paper cut-out men wearing identical pinstriped suits, bowler hats and briefcases strolling down the sidewalk, plunking their closed umbrellas alongside them like mountaineers scaling a cliff.

From the tearoom on the corner of Kings Road, the bustle of the city washes around me the way a fast-flowing river sweeps past a boulder. Sitting at my table, catching up on the news of the day over a freshly brewed pot of tea, I ponder-not for the first time-- how the world has changed. Not so long ago, to collect information one would visit places like pubs and the docks; notorious locations where men with loose lips are always happy to chat to an audience for the price of a drink. In ancient Rome you could sit in a bath house and learn more than if you sat in the senate all day, or going back even further, information was freely spread around a warm, protecting campfire. I have stood alongside humanity since they first painted an image on a cave wall and took that first step towards civilization, and I have learnt that no matter the age, no matter the medium, truths can be uncovered where people feel comfortable and safe.

Today, radio and television provide information and news with immediacy and intimacy, but as it often contains little more than highlights and no real gristle, it's all an illusion. For a real feast of what was happening in the world you still needed to read newspapers; and not just one, but as many as possible as each has their own style, focus and flavour.

Knowledge is like any garden. It must be worked, its fields tilled, seeds planted, and the soil nourished.

Today I begin with the lighter articles, but soon find myself caught up in the stories of the day. The first involved Mary Bell, an eleven-year-old killer who murdered two boys, aged three and four. She had been convicted of both murders, and the newspapers proclaimed the girl was a *"very grave risk to other children if not closely watched"*. The more liberal papers were also talking about Mary, pointing out she had not so much been sentenced as committed—and they admitted there was no suitable hospital or appropriate detention centre to house the young girl.

The second story catching everyone's attention was that Apollo 8 was preparing to leave the Earth and, for the first time ever, orbit the Moon. This miracle of science and engineering stood in stark contrast to the apparent, never-ending swell of human savagery that was Mary Bell. Thinking back to the first staggering steps humanity took in search of fire, warmth and protection to this day when they were about to orbit a new world, an uncontrollable smile spread across my face.

Since papyrus was first created, I have written down my journey with humanity, as they have grown from a small tribe of hunters and gatherers to planting their first crops and taking that important step towards self-determination. Soon that tribe would leave the earth and visit another celestial object for the first time.

This warmth melted away and was replaced by a chill down my spine when I read the next article. This was a small story from Cairo, reporting that a British archaeological team, led by Dr George Harrison (not of Beatles fame), had begun a forensic exploration of King Tutankhamen's mummified corpse. The story noted how, for a short time, the boy-kings head had been *removed and packed in a sugar box.

Devouring the article, it explained the archaeologists were blaming the condition of the mummy on Howard Carter's original team in 1918. These modern scientists had discovered that Tut's body was beginning to deteriorate because it had been left exposed for several years during the 1920s. They had also recorded at some point the limbs had been detached, most likely to remove any jewellery from the body during its original examination. The article explained the pharaoh's head had likely been detached to help remove the famous gold mask so prominently featured in the article's photo. The team also announced that after recognising a possible scalp wound, X-rays had revealed the presence of bone shards inside the skull. This led the Egyptologists to speculate that Tutankhamun had been murdered, likely by a blow to the head. I was the only person alive who knew the truth of Tutankhamun's death and why his head had been removed back during those long days in Egypt when I lived alongside his family, and this tale began with the death of his Grandfather, Amenhotep III and his uncle Djhutmose.

Hawara, 1348 BC

In a land dominated by plagues, this latest one was threatening to explode out of North Africa and destroy the entire world. The outbreak had first appeared in the south of the kingdom, but soon spread into neighbouring towns and cities. Entire regions of Egypt were wiped out, and men armed with silver-edged weapons and silver-tipped arrows began hunting the deadly Wepwawet. Though outwardly resembling a wolf, the hunched shoulders and strangely intelligent eyes revealed the true, demonic nature of these beasts.

Such creatures were dangerous to the unwary, but the men led by the Crown Prince Djhutmose—Overseer of the Priests of Upper and Lower Egypt, High Priest of Ptah in Memphis and eldest son of the Pharaoh, Amenhotep III—were far from unwary. Specifically trained for such encounters, with years of experience hunting the horrid creatures to cleanse their numbers from the countryside, Djhutmose had finally moved on the city at the epicentre of the outbreak. Home to the golden wolf-headed god Anubis, Cynopolis was where the Crown Prince had received word the true source of the Wepwawet plague was located. This move was expressly against his father's orders as the Pharaoh was weary of upsetting Anubis. The Pharaoh had gone even further and specifically asked me not to support his son's dangerous plan to confront one of the gods of the land.

Due to this order, I joined Djhutmose's attack in disguise. I had argued against such a move as taking on Anubis directly was folly. Still, I liked the price and wanted to be nearby in case I could offer assistance.

For this final battle against the plague, the Crown Prince was also backed by his younger brother, Prince Amenhotep, and together we had all fought and cut down Anubis and many of the Wepwawet that dwelled around Cynopolis. The battle cost us much, as amongst the many who fell under the claws of the werewolves was Djhutmose. He'd been clawed across his neck while facing Anubis himself, and I watched as the still living crown-prince was carried back to the capital by Prince Amenhotep.

The formal greetings were ignored as the king's messenger barged through the gathered priests and into my private quarters at Karnak.

I had been involved in the battle with Anubis against the Pharaohs wishes and did not want anyone knowing, so I had returned to my own compound before news of the fight arrived.

The Pharaoh's messenger fell to his hands and knees in veneration. "Oh, Great Amun, the king asks for your presence immediately."

"What's happened now? Has somebody seen something in the innards of a goat prophesising doom and gloom again?" Ok, I was a bit of an unpleasant god, but having people drop to their knees whenever you take a breath gets old real quick.

"My Lord?" the man asked, confused.

"What has happened?" I demanded. No sense of humour in these messengers.

"It's the Crown Prince, my Lord. He's dying."

I knew this was going to be trouble as the Pharaoh doted on his eldest son and he was going to ask me to do something I did not want to do. I stood up from my table and beckoned the messenger to lead the way. A chariot waited outside, and we both sped off to the palace of Amenhotep III.

The ride took almost no time, and arriving I was ushered past the crowd of kneeling Egyptians, reacting to my presence, and I forwent the usual plea for them to stand up as I acted out my concern for the boy. The people of the Nile saw me as a god. When you are near immortal and appear to possess unfathomable knowledge, these things get noticed. In my experience, they lead to either being stoned to death or worshipped as a god. The latter seemed to be the more comfortable choice.

I strode through the antechamber and walked directly into the royal family's private quarters. The palace guards were eyeing me nervously, but who was going to refuse entry to a god?

Once inside, I was shepherded to the Crown Prince's quarters. Here I found the family clustered about the bed containing the dying man. The Pharaoh looked up at my presence and gestured me forward to inspect his oldest son.

Back at the temple I could tell the gash across the neck was fatal, and looking now at the terrible ashen colour of the lad's skin, it was clear that he was not long for this world. I searched the dying boys face for any change in his features to indicate he'd been bitten by Anubis, and saw none. I had seen the fight and was certain Djhutmose had not been bitten, but when dealing with the unnatural it was always better to air on the side of caution.

I turned to Amenhotep III, a man I had known since his own birth four decades earlier. He returned my gaze with pleading eyes. He had always had a firm belief in my divinity, even taking my name as his own. As pharaoh, he had often sought and valued my council, and today he was asking me to save his son.

"What happened?" I asked, leaning forward to get a closer look at the neck wound.

"We were clearing away the last of the Wepwawet, and then entered the temple of Anubis." Prince Amenhotep said, looking down at his older brother.

"You entered at night?" I asked, playing out the charade.

Ignoring me, Amenhotep the younger went on. "We had cleared Cynopolis of all the children of Anubis, and had only one place to check as the possible source of the plague."

"Anubis mauled the Crown Prince before we arrived. It took all our might to fight off the god and save Djhutmose." Many in the room made symbols of protection with the blasphemy of this act.

"You killed Anubis?" I asked the Prince.

"We did. The head and body were incinerated, along with the children of Anubis we killed around the temple."

"And Kebechet?"

"We never saw her!"

I looked at Amenhotep III, who now refused to meet my gaze. "I warned you about attacking him directly like this before we knew exactly what was going on. Now you have the daughter of Anubis on the run, and who knows where she's hiding or how big a grudge she's carrying."

"Surely you know where she is," the Prince snarled, his anger palpable.

"Do you not think a god can hide from the view of another god, boy?" I snarled back.

Everyone was taken aback when the Pharaoh stepped up to his son and slapped him hard. "Remember who you are talking to!"

Amenhotep took the blow without a sound and refused to put a hand to his reddening cheek. He looked far from chastised; in fact he continued his attack, now turning his fury on his father.

"If your god is so powerful, ask him to save your beloved son.?"

This was getting dangerous. I could of course save the dying prince, but in saving him I would be committing an even greater atrocity.

The Pharaoh turned and finally looked me in the eye. The black makeup around his eyes had run from his tears. "Can you do it? Can you save him?"

"No." I said flatly.

"You cannot, or you will not?" Prince Amenhotep demanded.

I looked from father to son, weighing up my next answer. "I will not. The process of death has already begun, and much of his Ka is already preparing to leave. If I was to interrupt this process now I would condemn Djhutmose to a fate far worse than death. If I interfered now I would likely detach his Ba from the body, and it would be lost forever."

"So once again we ask for evidence of your divinity, and once again we get nothing but riddles and excuses," the Prince accused, continuing an old argument.

I took a step towards the younger Amenhotep, fighting the urge to even up the redness of his face by slapping the other cheek. "You get precisely what you ask for. You want to save your brother, then let him die peacefully and take him through the rites of the dead. You claim to love your brother, well mourn his loss and use his life as a symbol to improve the lives of your people. Stop looking to the gods to repair your own mistakes. We' are not servants of man, ready to change the river of life on a whim. If you truly want to do right by Djhutmose, help guide him through the Duat and to a life as a blessed spirit."

Complete rubbish of course, but generations of these sorts of questions had armed me with a number of such responses to explain why I never used my supposed powers.

"I could help." A voice claimed from a side door to the room.

The family turned and watched as my supposed wife entered, flanked by four of her acolytes.

"Stay out of this," I warned her.

Ignoring me, Maut sauntered over and stood before the Great Royal Wife. "My dear Queen Tiye, you can listen to the winds of reason from these men, or you can let me save your son."

Tiye looked torn, but ignored my shake of head in the negative. I gave it one last shot.

"You know any pact with her will only end in tragedy." Yea, that sounded pretty weak to me too.

"If you save him, I shall build temples to you across the kingdom," Tiye offered.

"I warn you, by accepting the help Maut is offering, you're condemning Djhutmose to a fate far worse than death."

The Pharaoh stepped between myself and his Queen. "Help or leave!"

"I will do neither," I said flatly. "This is going to end badly, and you will need me."

Maut picked up a goblet of wine and placed it on a table. She then stood in such a way that no one else could see what she was doing, no one except for me that is, and I believe she did that deliberately. With a deft move, she emptied a small vial she had been hiding into the wine.

"Do not do this," I mouthed as she picked up the goblet.

Walking past me, she whispered, "I got rid of Anubis and his whore daughter, and now I' am getting rid of you."

Even at her most spiteful, she was aware of the danger of letting anyone else know the source of our long life was our blood. This, however, was something different. Muat had the look of someone who was willing to beat everything on a single roll of the dice.

With a flourish, my 'wife' handed the goblet over to the Pharaoh's physician. "Have him drink every single drop of this. I have laid a spell on the liquid that will heal his wounds."

The physician looked to the Pharaoh, who gave his approval with a nod. The doctor sat on the side of the bed, lifted Djhutmose's head and\poured the liquid gently into his mouth. It took several tips of the goblet, but soon the cup was empty.

The effect was almost immediate, colour was returning to his skin and his minor wounds began to close. Everyone was so focused on the Crown Prince that they did not notice Maut slip out of the room.

When Djhutmose opened his eyes, it was obvious something was wrong. There was little intelligence there; instead there was an animal-like ferocity in his gaze. In an instant the boyish features of Djhutmose disappeared behind the sharper, stronger face of a predator, with two elongated teeth resembling the fangs of a serpent appearing between his lips.

"Look out," I yelled as the creature that had been Djhutmose transformed completely. Before anyone could react, the vampire reached up, grabbed his concerned father, and tore the Pharaoh's throat out.

The king managed to free himself and staggered back, his hands clutching at his ruined throat as though he could physically stop the blood gushing out between his fingers.

I was close enough to charge the creature as it rose from the bed, using my shoulder as a battering ram. The impact was like hitting a small tree, but I manage to send the vampire staggering sideways just as it was reaching for his mother.

The monster skittered across the floor, failing to gain purchase on the blood-slick marble. I was fumbling through Djhutmose's ruined clothing in search of a weapon as the vampire managed to get its feet under itself and leap at me. The creature sailed through the air, hands outstretched, only to be met with the sharp edge of Amenhotep's silver sword.

The Prince's blade slashed through his brother's cheek and shoulder. Barely slowing it down, the blow gave me enough time to find the Crown Prince's sword. Wielding the silver-edged weapon, I turned to face its former owner, who picked itself up and charged.

Amenhotep swung his weapon in wide, powerful strokes, trying to keep the approaching creature away. Outside, the warning calls of the doctor and Queen Tiye, who had escaped the room, were being answered by those of the palace guard.

With my foot, I sent a small bedside table sliding across the floor into the creature. With its legs entangled in the piece of furniture, I stepped in beside the Prince, and together we began slashing at the vampire with our swords.

Each time the monster tried to lunge at one of us, the other thrust forward with their sword, the silver blade cutting the beast. Though the metal alone could not kill it outright, the silver caused it great pain.

Time and again we thrust and parried with the former Crown Prince, managing to keep it away until more guards arrived. The first one with a spear charged forward and thrust the large blade into the vampire. Others then added their own weight to the weapon's shaft, helping to hold the struggling creature it in place.

Even so young a vampire had unnatural strength, and despite having three men holding the spear, the creature began pushing them backwards as it tried to pull its way along the spear shaft to get at them.

This all allowed Amenhotep to move around and drive his sword into his brothers back. I then screamed at the men holding the spear to let the creature push them out into a nearby courtyard. Walking backwards slowly to ensure they kept their footing, the moment the men hauled the vampire into the sunlight its body burst into flames and we could all finally let go.

Amenhotep stood next to me and raised his hands to the sun high above. "Aten has cleansed the world of this evil. Its great light truly is the bringer of life."

Not comprehending just what had happened in the mind of the future pharaoh, I agreed.

Queen Tiye ordered the Royal Guard to search the palace, while the army was instructed to comb the city, for Maut. It turns out my wife believed her ruse had managed to kill everyone, including myself, so she had not bothered to run. The Guard found her in her own temple being served by her priests, awaiting news on our deaths so she could move on the throne. Her plan was to begin shaping the empire with her vision for humanity, and if you knew Maut, you knew that was not going to be a great option for anyone except Maut.

While the guards surrounded my wife and her followers, the rest of us got busy with the grisly work of committing Djhutmose's body to the flames to ensure he did not regenerate. I later found out why he had been so strong so quickly. It was not just her blood that Maut had poured into the goblet, but the blood from a Wepwawet. As I had feared, the entire Wepwawet outbreak had nothing to do with Anubis, framing the werewolf had been just one step in Maut's attempt to rule Egypt.

Next, we carefully searched the Pharaoh's body for a bite mark. In a day of tragedy, the Queen was pleased to hear her husband did not have to be committed to the fire to ensure he did not turn into a one of the creatures. The body of Amenhotep III would be allowed to go through the funerary rights and placed in the tomb his workmen had been preparing for the last few years.

While this was occurring the army ensured no one escaped the temple of Maut, so when I walked up to the compound's ornate front door with Amenhotep, I expected someone would have been there to greet us. Instead we found the large gate closed, but a little muscle had it swinging open.

Inside we found the goddess sitting calmly on her altar, her legs dangling below, the way a little girl does when sitting on a high stool.

"Why?"

Maut looked at me like I was an idiot. "You ask me why? You, who never look for the adoration of the masses, and yet here you are, the highest of us al. For someone with a prestigious memory, you so easily forget that I once sat where you are. As Sekhmet I was adored; my advice sought out by kings and peasants alike."

"A position I am sure you despised as you hate people."

"It is amazing what you miss once it's gone," she said, with a shrug and a smile.

"Well, your yearning for a lost life means you will soon be missing your head," Amenhotep promised, his sword catching the light from the lamps inside the temple.

"Powerful words from the new Pharaoh. You can thank me anytime you like, by the way."

"Thank you? You killed my father and my brother. You almost killed me, as well as my mother, so why would I thank you?"

"You're the next pharaoh are you not? A position you never thought in your wildest dreams you could achieve without divine intervention . . ."

The Prince gave Maut a hard, cold look, ". . . and who says I ever wanted to be pharaoh?"

"Pfffttt . . ." Maut exclaimed as she picked up a small gold tube from the table before turning to faced me. "You really should leave now."

"And why is that?" I asked.

"Because just like you, old snake, my blood allows me to heal almost any wound—it just takes longer depending on the injury or infection."

"Meaning?"

"Meaning? Well there are two. The first is the elementary trick a magician learns, to reveal something with your right hand to ensure they are not looking at what you hold in your left."

"And the second?" the Prince asked.

"That there is a reason why they once called me Sekhmet."

I threw my sword at her, yelling, "Don't let her drink."

The sword struck the altar next to her leg and clattered away harmlessly.

Amenhotep reacted to my warning and rushed forward, his own weapon raised, but it was too late. Maut lifted the small vial, identical to the one she had poured into Djhutmose's goblet, and drank.

Maut rolled backwards off the table in a gymnastic flip and was immediately back on her feet. Already her features were changing, but they did not resemble those of a Wepwawet. Unlike those minor werewolves, her nose widened, and her eyes grew rounder and larger. Her face elongated, but instead of the long, sharp snout of a wolf she developed a broader, stumpier nose.

"She's turning into a lion?" Amenhotep cried out, backing away.

"Sekhmet was before your time. She was a warrior goddess with the features of a lioness."

The lion-faced woman before us smiled and lifted one fur-covered hand, flexing the digits. Enormous hooked claws protruded in and out with the motion, and through a mouth full of large, sharp teeth she growled, "I warned you to leave."

With feline grace Maut leapt onto the altar, her muscles flexing and rippling under the tawny hide now covering her body.

"I could have left, but then I would have missed seeing your face when this occurred." I said, then lifted my fingers to my mouth and whistled. At the far end of the room, a large door swung open, and through this strode Anubis and Osiris—the deity of the dead and resurrection. Anubis was only in partial werewolf form and he looked far from happy, having only just been revived by Osiris. His great wolf-head opened and a challenging howl erupted. The noise was almost painful in the confined space of the temple.

Once he was done, I turned back and smiled at Maut. "I made sure Anubis wasn't quite as dead as everyone assumed, and he was more than happy to come and help us out once I explained what you had done to him."

Unconcerned, the lioness shrugged in a very human manner at me, then snarled her own roar in response to the wolf's challenge.

Both monsters charged each other, with Maut scoring first blood when she raked the wolf across the snout with her clawed hand. Beads of blood tracked the passage of her blow as she reached back and tried to follow up with a second, but Anubis was far larger and was more comfortable in his animal form. He stepped into Maut's strike and wrapped his enormous arms around her. The werewolf then lifted her off her feet and, muscles bulging across his arms, shoulders and back, crushed the lioness in a formidable hug. Maut's head lifted back in a scream of pain and frustration, then sagged as her lungs were compressed in the crushing embrace. This motion allowed the wolf to bite down on her neck and shoulder. Blood splashed across both of them, and while Maut's attention was diverted, I retrieved my sword, snuck in and cut at her vulnerable legs.

Amenhotep caught on and began swinging at the other cat-like leg of Maut, and soon she was hamstrung and bleeding from a half a -dozen ugly cuts. I grabbed the Prince's shoulder and heaved him out of harm's way as the blood-soaked bitch wriggled and slid free from Anubis' grip. Already her wounds were healing, so the Prince and I darted forward again and struck at every point we could reach with our swords. A dozen heavily bleeding slashes across her body did little as she continued to struggle.

Thinking I had to do more, I admit I overreached when I thrust my sword deep into Maut's stomach. The attack meant I was now within arm's reach, and the lion-woman struck out at me with one large paw. Her claws cut deep across my face, and the blow sent me soaring backwards into a distant wall. She then managed to pull my sword from her body and throw it at Amenhotep, who dodged the missile easily.

Shaking the jolt off, I pulled myself back to my feet and watched as the hulking form of Anubis let go of Maut and, towering over her bloody body, punched down, his broad fist slamming into her face.

Even from where I stood I could hear bones crunch as the werewolf struck again and again, then after a few more punches he grabbed the lioness by the scruff of the neck and threw her into a stone pillar. Maut hit with a sickening thud but landed on her feet.

Amenhotep tossed me my discarded sword and we both went to work again, hacking and slashing with our weapons. Blood, fur and gore flew, yet still the lioness struggled on. The vitality of the woman was something to behold, not that I was thinking that at the time. I was afraid she was going to get up and kill us.

Luckily even the most unnatural creature has its limits, and soon Maut's struggles began to weaken as the power of her blood and the concoction she'd drunk wore off. The women slumped to the blood slick floor, though she was not dead yet. There was still enough poison in his veins to keep her alive. Amenhotep raised his sword to remove her head, and it was now when Osiris stepped into the fight and indicated he had a far better plan than simply killing her.

Things changed after the death of the Crown Prince.

It normally took seventy days for a body to go through the funeral rights and process of mummification, but due to the nature of Djhutmose's death and the burning of his body, this clearly could not happen. The problem was foregoing mummification would have brought forward some disturbing questions amongst the populace, so the proper rights were completed, there was even a coffin built. After the appropriate time this was placed deep in his father's yet to be closed tomb as Djhutmose, not having been a pharaoh, was not allowed to have his own tomb.

During those seventy days, while we remained and kept an eye on the destroyed body of Maut, the army was sent out to find those few acolytes of hers that had fled the city. Most were killed outright, but a few were captured and brought back.

Watching Muat's body, it was clear she was still alive and slowly healing. Some of the smaller wounds had closed, and a little colour had returned to her skin.

The Egyptians believed one punishment for those trying to enter the afterlife was to leave some of the organs intact within the dead body before mummification. In a final act of his revenge for his dead brother and father, Amenhotep took Osiris' suggestion that Maut go through only part of the mummification process, with her brain pulled out her nose by small hooks, but everything else was to remain. Oil from cedar trees was pumped into every organ and vein, to preserve the body and remove any fluids that could cause rotting and bloating. Wrapped in linen bandages, coated with a resin that was both waterproof and retarded fungal and microbe growth, Maut was then buried in Djhutmose's empty royal coffin, To ensure the end of the cult of Maut, the same was then done to her acolytes, both living and dead.

The burial celebration was held until the summer solstice, when the god Ra raised the sun through the lion constellation, known in the future as Leo. Further, they were all buried with the mummies of two lions. This all ensured the regal power of these predators were removed from Maut and returned to the royal family, while the celestial power of the lion constellation and the growing belief in the sun's power within the new Pharaoh, kept her undying body in place.

With her ability to slowly heal, Maut's body would try to regenerate itself, though the total lack of brain meant there was nothing to reform. Meanwhile the infused cedar oil would continually poison the organs and all but kill Maut over and over again.

When these Egyptians took their revenge, they did not mess around.

About the Author:

Phil's worked at London's Natural History Museum, the Field Museum in Chicago, the Smithsonian's National Museum of Natural History as well as Australia's National Dinosaur Museum, the Australian War Memorial, Questacon, National Film and Sound Archives, the Australian National Botanic Gardens. Published in newspapers and magazines across the globe, including the world's longest running dinosaur magazine, The Prehistoric Times and Famous Monsters of Filmland. 2020 sees the release of his WW1 trench murder mystery, 'Golgotha'.

His first novel 'Brotherhood of the Dragon' *contains another Amun adventure and these always contain true history facts (with some embellishments). Amenhotep III and his oldest son did die under mysterious circumstances . . . though there's a suggestion Djhutmose left Egypt and became the basis of the Moses story. With his death his younger brother, Amenhotep IV, became Pharaoh and mysteriously moved Egypt away from the worship of Amun to the lesser god Ra, whose giant fiery ball rose and fell every day. Amenhotep IV changed his name to reflect his belief in the power of the Aten to Akhenaten, and his heir was Tutankhaten. The worship of Aten annoyed many Egyptians, and things got so bad that when he finally died, Akhenaten's heir took the throne and to appease everyone, returned the original gods to their former glory and took the name Tutankhamun.*

NOTE: This short story appears in a modified version from the larger story in the upcoming sequel to the Amun Galeas Bloodline trilogy.

Orphan Days

Neen Cohen

She flicked through the pages of the magazine, trying to ignore the mother screaming at her child while a teenager coughed into a ripped tissue that stopped nothing.

The carpet of the old doctor's surgery had been pulled up since her last visit. The floorboards did nothing to improve the dilapidated house turned surgery.

"Nila." Doctor Fraser's quiet voice floated over to the small waiting area.

Nila happily dropped the magazine back on to the coffee table, leaving it open at the star signs, now six months out of date. It might at least have been interesting had she known her actual birthdate.

"Hey, Doc."

Doctor Fraser smiled and nodded to the chair opposite her. They both sat on the one side of the dark wooden desk. It was pushed up against the one window in the room and only used when the doctor was alone. "Good morning Nila. How have you been doing?"

"I'm okay, Doc."

"No more self-harming?"

Nila closed her eyes. There was no point saying the recent cuts on her stomach weren't her own doing. They never believed her. She shook her head and smiled, with closed mouth and clenched teeth.

"Then how can I help today?"

Nila never saw the Doc without a smile and—depending on her mood—it either comforted or frustrated the hell out of her. "I just need a new script."

"Of course." She picked up the old pad sitting on the coffee table beside a stained mug and began writing.

"It would be easier if you just used the computer."

"Perhaps one day, when my fingers no longer hold the pen," Doctor Fraser said, passing the paper to Nila.

"Thanks, Doc."

"If they stop working, make sure you come back."

"Of course."

But they had stopped working months ago.

Her hand on the doorknob, Nila almost breathed a sigh of relief. Too soon.

"Nila, have you gotten rid of it?"

Nila forced a smile on her lips and turned back to the doctor, lifting her shirt as she did. Her skin felt bare where the small pocketknife usually rested in the band of her shorts.

Doctor Fraser nodded a dismissal.

Nila walked out, the small knife pressing hard against the inside of her right ankle.

She breathed deeply of the scorching air. The thin light shirt stuck to her skin; her shorts barely touched the top of her thighs. But no matter the heat, she wouldn't stop wearing her boots.

Taking her time, Nila walked down the road, the sound of the waves crashing against the golden beach to her right.

Very few people were out on the streets, and those few raced to-and-fro between air-conditioned cars and air-conditioned shops and offices.

She loved the working week. It was the weekends that were a nightmare. No matter how hot, tourists came to have their getaway, breathing in the sea air as though an hour here could fix their drudgery of work, eat, sleep, and repeat that made up their Monday to Friday.

The biting sun reflected off every shiny object.

Nila slipped on her sunglasses and continued her dawdle down to the chemist.

The script never took long to fill. As though the chemist was scared to delay; eager to get Nila out before something terrible happened.

It had been like that since she first washed up on shore. Three or four years old, raging with fever and uncontrollably thrashing her arms and legs.

She had woken strapped to a bed, no memory of before.

Yet they were the ones who were scared of her.

She didn't remember hurting the people who were tried to save her. But it would torment her childhood and adolescence anyway.

They called her a beast. A raging, uncontrollable beast.

And when it got too much, she proved them right.

She took a deep breath of the sun's blistering anger and it washed through her like a drink of cold water.

"Have a good day," said Mr Phillip Jenkins, father to the biggest bully in the town. He was the only chemist.

Nila bit the inside of her cheeks to stop herself from laughing at the beads of sweat on his forehead, despite the air-conditioning.

"You too, Phillip." She smiled sweetly as she snatched the newly filled bottle of pills.

His eyes narrowed.

The pills had stopped working.

Every time Nila went to see Doctor Fraser it was with the intentions of letting her know.

Three bottles now rattled around in the bottom of her dirty frayed messenger bag.

She groaned as the clouds built, the heat increased, and the world darkened. The pressure building inside of her, mirrored by nature.

Maybe just another few pills, maybe they will work today.

She dry swallowed but they did nothing.

Her blood continued to run hot in her veins and she still saw the lion-headed beasts when she turned every other corner.

Her imaginary friends that had never gone away.

Sekky and Nut.

Sometimes she could almost hear what they were discussing. Words hidden beneath the growls and roars.

As she walked towards the end of the main strip of shops, she saw them laying on the grass strip between the road and the sea. Lithe bodies dressed in robes, one white and one red, both adorned with golden accessories. They glinted in the light.

Nut had straight black hair, while Sekky's mane, sunshine and fire, sparked with each movement.

As a child no-one was too surprised or concerned about her imaginary friends, not until she spoke of their lion heads and their claws. As a child Sekky and Nut protected her, until she got angry with them instead of everyone else.

The anger continued to build up inside of her as she rubbed the scratches Sekky had given her in their last argument.

The anger was always building; it was always there.

The pills would help.

Why had the pills stopped working?

The heat of the day continued to press against her skin, moisture floating on the very air. Nila felt herself burning from the inside out as she crossed the road toward the water.

Her lionesses drew closer, their words a buzzing, a wave crashing against the shore.

The hand was hot and heavy as it landed on her shoulder.

Fuelled by anger, she turned, fist clenched.

She slammed her fist into the face before she saw it.

Peter's bulbous nose began to bleed.

Nila stared for a moment, then the smell of the blood hit her nose.

When she finally walked away from Pete, curled in a foetal position on the sidewalk her hands were red.

They were chatting and laughing. Those imaginary friends turned foes.

Her rage held no bounds.

Electricity raced beneath her skin as she grabbed the front of their robes, half expecting her hands to simply pass through.

"Who are you?" She growled.

"We are your parents." Nut's voice was thunder on the wind as she flicked her ebony hair from her shoulders.

"You are our favourite creation. Mixing my anger and her power. Such a perfect child." Sekky's voice was always deeper, her red robes flowing around her like a bloody river.

"Child?"

"We are your goddesses. We saved you on that beach. You were reborn with our light. And you have now come into your full potential."

"My anger?"

"So beautiful. So pure." They spoke together.

Nila's nostrils flared. Her hands pushed against their chests as she let the silken material go. In one movement, without thought, she crouched and pulled the knife from her boot.

She smiled as they cocked their hands.

She moved.

A circle, a dance.

Their blood spilled from their gaping necks.

Nila walked away, not waiting to see their bodies collapse and stain the grass with their blood.

She remembered their full names. Sekhmet and Tefnut.

She was a child reborn of the Lion, an August morning washed up on shore.

Her parents died as she walked away.

She was their child.

She preferred being an orphan.

About the Author:

Neen Cohen is an LGBTQI and speculative fiction author. She's been published through several publishers including Black Hare Press, Little Quail Press, Camden Park Press, and NBH Publishing. She has a Bachelor of Creative Industries and is a member of the Springfield Writers Group.

Neen lives in Brisbane Australia with her partner, son and fur babies. She loves to roam cemeteries, botanic gardens, and construction sites and can often be found writing while sitting against a tree or tombstone.

Check out her latest adventures and upcoming publications over on her Blog: https://wordbubblessite.wordpress.com

Night of the Lion

Deeanna West

Golden rays split the still dark sky creating a silhouette of everything in the foreground. The soaring branches of the boabs lining the ridge were the dark smudges of an oil painting. I squinted, forcing my eyes to focus. There. Movement. I raised my arm to point, directing everyone's attention between the trees. They tittered, whispering to each other that they couldn't see, that there was nothing there, but I ignored them. They'd see what I had seen, and soon.

The sharp intake of five sets of tourists' breaths announced the second they saw them. The lions. It was a small pride, but they were reliable. Every morning at daybreak they rose, meandering down to the waterhole without a care in the world. They were used to the jeeps, used to the staring of safari-goers desperate to tick lion off their big five lists.

"Nick, can we get closer?" one of the tourists whispered.

I glanced to her. Blonde hair hacked off around her ears and eyes hidden behind sunglasses too big for her face. I was terrible with names. There were too many people passing through and as head ranger I didn't usually run tours or interact with the guests all that much. The only reason I was running this one was because Larkin was sick. As it was, I'd just get the hang of a group and then they'd be gone again. Their spots filled with fresh faces I had to learn all over again. It was odd for me to remember hers so clearly. Bridgette. When Griggs had announced he was taking on a vet student we'd all been shocked. He was a cranky bastard and was more likely to make a student cry than teach them anything. If she survived him, she'd be a great vet.

"Just wait," I replied to Bridgette's question.

As if summoned by my words, he approached. Abioye. He stalked towards our jeep with all the arrogance of a creature that knew he was king. He left the females to stand before us, glaring at us, pretending that he may pounce at any moment. He wouldn't of course. I met his eye. My green to his deep golden. We understood each other, he and I. Seven years he'd ruled this area. For seven years I'd watched him grow into the magnificent specimen that commanded the attention of all.

"He's stunning," Bridgette gushed, camera forgotten in her grasp. "What is he, 100, 200 kilos?"

"About a hundred and ninety, yeah."

She nodded to herself and I wondered what she was thinking. I almost asked but her attention had already returned to Abioye so I turned back to the staring tourists.

"Every morning Abioye and his pride make this trek to the waterhole. It's the best time to get close to them. For those that are interested, there's a hide by the water's edge. Three people can go at daybreak tomorrow and get a close view of the pride. You'll most likely see some wildebeest and gazelle as well."

"Oh yes, I want to do that! Mum, can we do that?" The youngest of the tourists asked. Just turned sixteen, she and her mother had booked this safari to celebrate. Abbi. That was it. Why could I remember their stories so much easier than their names?

Her mother nodded. "If you can drag yourself out of bed early enough, then we can."

"Ugh mum, come on."

Smiling, I restarted the jeep. "Come on troops, it's time for breakfast."

Bridgette smiled at me across the table, plate loaded with bacon and coffee balancing precariously as she dragged a chair across with a foot.

I raised an eyebrow at her. "I would have thought a vet student would be all about the veggies."

"Oh, heaps of girls in my class are vegetarian, but I'm not one of them. I mean, what kind of psycho can turn their nose up at bacon?" She accentuated her words by taking a huge bite and smiling as egg yolk dripped down her chin.

A laugh escaped me. "You're an animal."

"I'll fit right in here then."

She wasn't wrong. It could get pretty wild here sometimes. Between the morning rounds of the park and the tourist parties that went late and kept everyone awake, there were some days I only got a few hours sleep.

"So how long is your placement?"

"Three weeks."

I whistled. "Three weeks with Griggs. You're a brave woman."

"He's been great so far. He's like a superstar of wildlife medicine. There's so much I can learn from him and his reference for internships is like a golden ticket."

"I don't doubt that there's a lot he can teach you. Just don't take his crap personally ok?"

She frowned. "What do you mean."

"Griggs can be a little, grumpy is all."

"I see. Well I think I can handle myself, so don't you worry."

My eyes drifted down to my empty plate. I'd come in early to avoid the rush for the buffet having learnt the hard way not to get between someone's great aunt and the chocolate chip pancakes. From downcast eyes I watched Bridgette eat, I had no reason to hang around but I wanted to stay and talk with her. Time had caught up with me, I needed to go and she was probably expected at the clinic.

As if she was reading my mind Bridgette spoke around her food. "So, Nick, can I count on you being here for dinner tonight?"

I nodded. "Can't wait."

Unease settled hot in my gut and I frowned as I watched as the lionesses paced through the grass.

"Something disturbs them," Jaafan stated.

"But what?"

Jaafan had spotted them on his return from the tree tents and found me at once. As head ranger all the staff knew to find me if they noted anything out of the usual with the animals. Since his main job was to transport the tourists to and from the tree tents Jaafan was always watching out for the park as he drove. Since the park was so small, everyone was expected to help where they were able to and everyone had some basic training with firearms. The last time the pride was this distressed, poachers had cut through the fences, so I appreciated Jaafan coming with me now. An extra set of eyes to keep watch could be invaluable.

At this time of day, the pride sought shelter from the noon heat beneath the acacia on the edge of the reserve. To see them milling around now was concerning.

"You think poachers again?" Jaafan's black skin seemed flushed from the heat and worry marred his usually cheerful face.

"I don't think so," I replied. "The guys didn't report any problems this morning after their rounds. No cut fences or campfires. No, something else is going on."

Frowning, Jaafan inched the rover closer. The lionesses eyed us but didn't move away.

"Where's Abioye?"

Jaafan shook his head. "I haven't seen him since yesterday."

"He was around this morning when I took the group out for Larkin." As I spoke, I turned and fished the binoculars off the back seat. I scanned the pride, but the big male was nowhere to be seen.

"I don't think he's—" I bit off my words as I spotted on a tan shape lying still in the grass. "There!"

Jaafan drove where I indicated, beeping the horn in an effort to drive the lionesses away. Leaving Jaafan to keep watch and handing him my rifle, I approached the body. Abioye didn't move and for a moment I worried he was already dead. His chest rose in a ragged breath and hope replaced the dread I'd been feeling.

"He's still alive! Call the other rangers and Griggs."

Jaafan leapt to obey, shouting down the two-way that we needed a transport vehicle and Griggs. Even with Abioye unconscious it wasn't safe to try and move him without more hands and sedatives.

"Hang in there buddy," I whispered to the unconscious lion. "We got you."

It took four of us to stretcher Abioye into the small veterinary clinic beside the resort. The moment we heaved him onto the treatment table, Griggs started yelling, causing the others to flee the room.

"Get a catheter in!" Griggs snapped at a nurse. His hands were already busy, drawing blood from Abioye's jugular as a second nurse fought to keep his head raised.

She was struggling, Abioye's head was a dead weight and she was a petite thing. I hadn't been told to leave so I stepped into the room to help her. The nurse, Izzy I think, nodded her thanks and hurried to press an oxygen mask to the big cat's face.

"Catheter's in."

"Good. Run this blood." Griggs shoved the tubes to Bridgette. "Full health profile and bring in the results as soon as they're ready."

As Bridgette leapt to obey, Griggs drew a clear liquid from a small glass vial. He flicked the bubbles out before injecting the liquid into the catheter. "Hold his head up again."

I obeyed, hefting Abioye's head up by the scruff and a lip, watching in awe as Griggs shoved a tube down his throat. I'd watched Griggs work before of course. Seen his clean sutures on Hamlet, the cook's dog, after it had tried to chase a baboon away from the bins. But seeing him working now, a solid block of calm amidst the chaos of the emergency room was a whole other thing. Even though he was a stuck up prick any other time, I couldn't help but be impressed.

Bridgette raced back in and handed Griggs some papers. His eyes scanned the document, lips moving as he read.

"What's wrong with him?" I asked, unable to stop myself.

Griggs sighed and looked straight at me. "His white cell count is almost non-existent, he's anaemic and his globulins are tanked. Fluid in his abdomen. I'd have to send bloods to the lab to be one hundred per cent sure, but I'd put money on this being FIP."

It wasn't a disease I'd heard of before. We'd had reports of Distemper and Babisiosis killing lions but there'd been no sign of that here.

Griggs must have seen the confusion on my face. "Feline Infectious Peritonitis. Nasty disease. Abioye doesn't fit the textbook case but I'm pretty sure. He has all the indicators." A brief pause as he connected a fluid line. "I'll do my best to support him, maybe even get him up and going again. But Nick, it's a band aid, this will catch up to him eventually. And that's *if* he survives the night."

I nodded, throat tight. Abioye wasn't a pet, he didn't belong to me, yet seven years watching him rule his pride had created a bond. Swallowing hard, I tried to be practical. "Do what you can but we can't let him suffer. Better to put him to sleep than let him suffer and die out there on the plains."

"That's a good way to look at it," Griggs agreed. "Now get out of my surgery and let me do my job."

I obeyed, pausing as Bridgette placed a hand on my arm.

Her eyes were sympathetic. She'd almost certainly seen this before as a student, seen the grieving owner receiving the news that there was no hope.

I tried to smile. This was Africa after all, I'd seen death before and would again.

The sound of flesh hitting stainless steel drew our attention before I could leave.

"Shit!"

The expletive broke through Grigg's cool demeanour as he lunged for the vials of medications on the shelf above the table.

Abioye's body thrashed, held on the table only by the nurses leaning on him. Legs kicked despite whatever drugs Grigg's administered.

I couldn't move, rooted to the spot as the shit hit the fan. It was for the best though, I'd just get in the way. Everything moved in fast forward, everyone fighting to regain control until, with a strained silence, it all just stopped. Abioye's body fell still, no residual tremors or rise of the chest to mark his life.

Griggs pressed his stethoscope to his chest but almost straight away shook his head. "He's gone."

I nodded, but was unable to speak past the lump in my throat.

"I'll take care of his body," Griggs offered.

He understood and it was a god send.

Bridgette caught up as I escaped down the hall. "Hey, are you ok?"

I just stared at her.

"Right, silly question. He was a magnificent animal, I'm so sorry he died." She paused and laid a hand on my arm. "Do you want to go see if there's any ice cream? Or Bacon? Something tasty might make you feel a little better?"

My mouth twitched. Almost a smile, this woman was something special. "I'm ok without the food. Thanks for the offer though. I was thinking that I need to go on patrol, check the rest of the pride, make sure none of the others are sick. Usually Griggs would come but maybe he'd be happy for you to instead?"

"Right, good thinking. Give me two seconds to check with Griggs and then I'll come with you."

I waited as she disappeared around the corner, not really believing that Griggs would let her come. She bounced back again and this time I let myself smile. Griggs must think highly of her if he was letting her come instead of himself.

We walked in silence until we got out to the rover. Jaafan was leaning against it, arms crossed and chewing jerky. He snapped to attention as we approached, waiting for an update. I shook my head. "He didn't make it."

Swearing under his breath, Jaafan kicked at the dirt. "So what do we do now?"

"We're heading out to check the girls. Make sure none of them are sick."

"Call me if there's something?"

"Of course." I agreed.

Tyres spun on the dirt road as I tried not to shower him in dust as we left. Within the clinic it had felt like mere minutes had passed but the outside world had continued as scheduled. The afternoon sun blurred the horizon, but I was used to it. Used to the way you had to squint to focus. The lionesses hadn't moved from where they had found Abioye. Their pacing had stopped but they still seemed watchful.

"They look well enough," Bridgette whispered. She had the binoculars pressed so tight against her face an indent was forming.

"They do. But so did Abioye this morning."

We watched until the sun had begun to set, and the chill had me pulling on a jacket.

"We'll keep checking them but for now they seem ok. Let's head back." I said as I started the car.

Bridgette just nodded. There was nothing else we could do.

I didn't need to walk Bridgette back to the clinic, but it seemed like the polite thing to do. She had come with me to check the lionesses because she knew I was sad, after all. Shadows extended across the path as the sun set. Bridgette didn't know her way around well yet, so I directed her as the solar powered lanterns lining the paths gradually switched on.

"Do you still want to meet up for dinner?" she asked.

"I can just wait for you and we can go now." The sun had set on our way home and--despite everything--my stomach was making its hunger known.

Bridgette nodded. "Just let me get my jacket."

She disappeared into the clinic and I leant against a wall to wait. Shadows flickered at the end of the corridor where a light had blown and I briefly wondered if maintenance had been called.

A piercing scream snapped my attention from the busted light. I stormed into the clinic ready to fight a monster, or a poacher. Instead, I found Bridgette collapsed on the floor, hands pressed tight against her mouth. Blood oozed from a pile of flesh in front of her. Flesh that had been torn to pieces. The scent of the blood made me gag. The scattered scraps of blue fabric were all too familiar. Griggs.

I fought to swallow the bile threatening to rise in my throat, I leant in closer. An arm had vicious claw marks extending down the forearm. Instruments were strewn across the floor and Abioye's body was nowhere to be seen. We'd been gone for a while, but still Abioye should still be there. Griggs was going to perform a necropsy on him.

"I think Abioye did this." My voice sounded strained even to my ears, but it dragged Bridgette's attention away from Griggs mutilated body.

She shook her head. "The scratches look like they are from a lion, but this violence. It's like a frenzied attack. A lion wouldn't do this."

"There's no other explanation," I argued. "Look, I don't want to believe it either. Maybe the illness made him act irrationally? I don't know."

"What do we do?" Bridgette asked, regaining her feet.

"We have to make sure everyone is safe. Get the tourists back to their rooms. Then we find Abioye."

As a rule, we didn't carry our rifles around the villas. But I hadn't had a chance to stash the gun in my room since we got back. For once I was grateful for its weight slung across my back. I drew it as we headed out. I was loathe to shoot Abioye but if he had killed Griggs. Panic at being trapped in a small room and illness may have disoriented him, but it meant nothing. I wouldn't have any more lives lost today. If I could, I'd force Abioye back out into the park but if it came to it, I'd shoot.

We inched through the building, making our way towards the sleeping quarters. Most people would have headed to the tree tents at this time of the evening. But anyone here would be in the dining hall. Still, the bedrooms were closer.

"Mum, are you out here?"

Abbi stepped out of a room as we rounded the corner. I started to order her back inside when he appeared.

Abioye stared at us, eyes unblinking and clouded. He didn't move, no muscle twitches or the rise and fall of his chest as he breathed.

"Abbi," I hissed. "Get back in your room."

She whirled to obey but Abioye was faster.

He lunged with claws outstretched and mouth open wide. Fangs sunk into Abbi's neck as his jaw snapped shut. Red sprayed against the wall and her scream became a gurgle. With practiced efficiency the lion shook his head and Abbi went limp.

I didn't scream. Shock had driven the air from my lungs.

Abioye tore into Abbi's lifeless body, not feeding, just ripping her to shreds.

"Nick, the gun."

Now was our chance to put him down. At this close a range I wouldn't miss. Since his head was turned away, I aimed for his heart. Cracks split the air as I fired three times in quick succession, and the scent of gunpowder burnt acrid. The bullets sunk deep into Abioye's chest, decimating muscle and lung tissue to leave gaping holes in their wake. Undeterred the big lion continued to work, unconcerned by the kill shot I'd just delivered.

"Oh lord help us. The wounds, they aren't bleeding."

Those bullets would have torn through so many vital structures Abioye should be gasping on the floor, not turning to face us.

"Run!" Bridgette shrieked but I needed no prompting.

I'd never run so fast in my life. My lungs screamed in protest, but I just kept pumping my legs.

Bridgette's lithe form was already reaching an open guest room.

The clinking of Abioye's claws as they scrambled to find purchase on the tiles drove me forward. The thought of those nails tearing through flesh made me cringe.

As he rounded the corner, legs sliding out from under him, his great bulk slammed into the wall. In an instant, he rebounded and continued his charge towards us.

Bridgette threw the door shut behind me. The wood bucked as Abioye collided with it. Somehow the lock held, but I doubted it would survive more hits like that.

Scraping filled the room as Bridgette pushed a bookshelf across to reinforce the door. She was struggling, but fear kept me rooted in place--what if my weight was helping the door not give in?

She got the shelf close enough for me to help wedge it into position before we collapsed in front of it.

"What the hell is going on?" I hissed.

"I have a theory." She was hesitant, whispering to the floor without looking at me. Whatever she was about to say scared her. "Those bullets should have killed him. But did you see it? There was no blood. And I don't think he was breathing either. We saw him die in the clinic."

"Grigg's must have saved him after all," I interrupted.

"I don't think so. I think he's still dead." She took a deep breath. "Look I know this is going to sound crazy, but I think Abioye is a zombie. The walking dead. Hungry for brains. Whatever you like, but it explains the lack of blood and the change in behaviour."

I couldn't help it. I laughed. "You watch too much telly."

She frowned at me. "No, seriously, think about it. We watched him die. Now he's back killing everything he sees in a most un-lion way, doesn't breathe, doesn't bleed. This is the truth. The FIP must have mutated somehow."

The word seemed to echo around the room. Zombie. It was ridiculous, insane and yet now that it had been put forward, it made sense.

"Ok, let's say he's a zombie lion."

"He is," Bridgette asserted.

"So, we have a zombie lion roaming through a safari park. Most of the tourists are at the tree tents with Jaafan. They're safe. But there are a few still here. Abbi's mum, Lorraine."

Bridgette frowned. "And the Clines."

"And Frank, Livia and Bisa. All the rest of the staff live off-site so they'll be ok."

"We have to trap him. Stop him hurting anyone else and stop him escaping," Bridgette said.

"We're going to need help."

I nodded then pressed my ear against the wall. Silence. There was no way to be sure, but we had to get out of this room. Hopefully the quiet was real and Abioye had moved on. Heart pounding, I pushed the bookshelf aside and opened the door a crack. The hallway was empty.

"Where do you think he went?" Bridgette whispered.

Abioye had only hit the door twice in his attempt to get to us.

"I know what you know," I replied. "Chances are he's lurking just around a corner."

"That's a pleasant thought."

"Somehow we have a zombie lion. I think pleasant is long gone."

She nodded and started walking down the hall. Or maybe creeping would be more accurate. I felt like I was inching my way along the hall rather than walking. On a normal day, the gun slung over a shoulder was enough to make me feel safe. Just the sound of it discharging was enough to scare most predators away. Yet now the weapon was useless to me.

The smell hit us first. Metallic. We both recognised it as we approached a t-section in the corridor. Blood seeped across the floor to our left. Abioye was nowhere to be seen but the mess he'd left behind was fresh. Limbs lay strewn separate from the body and one blank eye stared up at me, the other mutilated with scratches. I couldn't stop it this time. My stomach clenched and purged itself.

Embarrassed, I wiped my mouth with my sleeve.

"Sorry," I apologised to Bridgette.

She didn't seem to have noticed, eyes fixated on the body. "Who is she?"

"Livia. The housekeeper"

"I'm so sorry, Livia," Bridgette whispered before turning to me. "We need to keep going."

I followed her down the right corridor, towards the dining hall. The faint thrum of chatter greeted us, but it was quieter than usual with everyone at the tree tents. As soon as we entered, I called for attention. I had no idea what I was going to say. How did you explain a zombie lion was terrorising the villa without sounding insane?

"This is going to sound crazy, but I need you all to listen to me," I started. "One of the lions has contracted a serious illness. He passed away, but somehow, he's come back. I shot him but it had no effect. Now I know what I'm about to ask is going to be hard, but I need your help. Our best option is to trap Abioye in the walk-in freezer. Its large enough and strong enough to contain him."

The Clines nodded without hesitation. From memory they were an action seeking couple on their anniversary. They'd spent the last one climbing mount Everest. I indicated they should follow me, leaving Bridgette to speak with Lorraine, Abbi's mum.

I ran through the plan with the others but couldn't help watching Bridgette. She spoke too softly for me to hear. How did you even tell a mother that her daughter had been murdered by a lion? Lorraine's face went pale in an instant and her eyes widened. She sank down in her chair, her hand clasped over her mouth. Bridgette wrapped her arms around her, holding her. Truth be told I'd expected screaming, but it seemed Lorraine's grief was the silent type of streaming tears and withdrawing from the world. My heart ached for her.

"Wait here," I told the Clines, turning my attention away from the mother's pain.

They obeyed and I slipped into the kitchens. As expected, Frank and Bisa were huddled in the back over a small fold-out table. Cards lay strewn, in the middle of a game. They started as I approached. Harvey the chef hated them gambling in the kitchens. They'd been on the receiving end of his rants more than once. It was unusual for them to take the risk so soon after dinner. Harvey could return any moment.

"It's ok, just me."

"Nick, nice to see you. What is happening?" Greeted Bisa.

I started to fill them in when the radio crackled.

"This is Jaafan. We require immediate assistance at tree camp, over."

"Jaafan its Nick. What's going on."

"Nick, it's the lionesses, they've gone crazy. They killed Harvey. He came to deliver more dessert and they killed him. Oh lord they killed him."

Jaafan's sobs were clear. I longed to help him but there was nothing I could say that would make this better.

"Listen to me, Jaafan. The same thing's happening to Abioye. Guns don't work. You have to stay in the trees."

The crackle of the radio was my only reply. "Jaafan? Jaafan? What's happening?"

Nothing. Shit.

I couldn't dwell on whatever was happening at tree camp, could only hope everyone would stay safe within the branches. Saving the people here had to happen first.

"Is everyone in place?" I asked.

A chorus of 'yes' and a 'roger that' from Frank was my reply. I took a deep breath, trying to quell the shaking in my hands. Chances were, I would die in about a minute. Right. Well, no point in delaying.

The freezer doors stood wide, sheltering everyone behind them. A pile of microwaved meat lay in a steaming heap in the centre of the room. The bait. Well, the second lot of bait that I hoped would command Abioye's attention once he was in the freezer. I turned my attention to the large ornate double doors of the dining room. We'd created a path from those doors, through the kitchen to the freezer. Our trap.

Not a squeak announced the opening of the doors. Not what I needed. I took a deep breath then screamed. Loud and long I kept screaming. Hopefully, I sounded like a wounded animal. Like prey.

I heard him coming. The heavy pad of his paws as he moved towards me. The second he rounded the corner and spotted me, I ran.

Abioye followed.

At the freezer door I turned to face my killer. This was it. Abioye leapt, a solid wall of muscle and teeth. I collapsed onto the floor letting the momentum of his pounce carry him into the freezer. Pain seared across my shoulder and then I was moving. Yanked sideways by Bisa as planned. Our timing was perfect. As soon as I was clear everyone set shoulders against their door, heaving them shut. The gap closed as Abioye eyed the meat we had left him. How was I alive?

Our meat bribe wasn't enough.

"Push!"

I leapt forward to help, but we were too slow. The closing doors jerked to a stop as Abioye forced his shoulder and arm through the gap. His body trapped within the freezer he clawed at the metal, trying to pull the rest of his bulk through the door. I grunted, white fire burning down my side where his claws must have cut me, but I couldn't stop. If he got out. No.

"Keep pushing!"

We strained and someone cried. Abioye's claws scrambled for enough purchase to push his way free. The doors gave and Abioye launched into the room.

Frank screamed as a swipe of Abioye's paw opened his abdomen to spill intestines on the floor. Glistening coils covered in blood that held my gaze despite Mr Cline crumbling beneath the lion in my peripheral.

"Come on, come on!" Bridgette screamed as she grabbed at my arm. The panic in her voice snapped me back to attention.

Mrs Cline went down trying to save her husband as we fled, Bridgette towing Lorraine with me and Bisa following behind.

"Which way?" Bridgette asked, letting me take the lead.

"The cars," I replied.

A crash drove us faster. We could hear him, upending tables in his pursuit.

"He's coming," sobbed Lorraine, over and over again. She provided the soundtrack to our panic.

Bursting into the night and seeing the cars parked before us brought tears to my eyes. "Get Lorraine in the rover," I yelled to Bridgette.

She didn't break stride, just veered towards the vehicle as I ran towards the lockbox for the keys.

Keys in hand, I turned back. Abioye loomed in the doorway, clearly lit within the golden pool of light spilling across the threshold.

Hearing the lion, Bisa turned, with terror written upon on his face. The movement unbalanced him, feet twisting as he fell. He hit the ground hard, crying out in pain and then horror as Abioye descended on him. Blood sprayed, collecting in Abioye's coat.

The car. I had to get to the car. I covered the ground in a few strides and vaulted into the vehicle. It started the first time and the relief had me sobbing. The tyres skidded on the road, but I didn't care. It didn't matter, we were alive.

"He's gone," Bridgette stated. She was twisted in her seat, looking back on the villa, one hand still clutching Lorraine's as she sobbed.

I just nodded. There was nothing there to keep him. Everyone was dead.

"What's going to happen now?" Bridgette asked.

"I don't know," I replied.

As we lapsed into a tense silence a roar exploded in the night around us. Though we sped away it felt like it was right outside. Another roar sounded in reply, further away but no less powerful. Fear tightened my knuckles on the steering wheel. Fuck. I reached for the radio, praying Jaafan's earlier unresponsiveness had just been radio error.

"Jaafan, it's Nick. Are you safe?"

The radio crackled but no voice answered my call. The sound echoed around the car and my stomach clenched. There would be no help there.

About the Author:

Deeanna West is a fantasy author writing from sunny north Queensland. If a book has magic, strange and amazing creatures or a world completely different to our own, then she's sold. When not holed up writing, she can be found playing games on the Xbox or out riding her horse.

THIS IS THE DAWNING (PART VIII)

Helena McAuley

Leo's arrogance is unapologetic. Despite this, I have always liked him, though some others of the Twelve find him distasteful. What they don't realise is that, in order to work with Leo, you must meet his arrogance head-on and not bow to it. Only then will he respect you.

I, personally, have never found this to be a problem.

Douglas and I walk into the Her Majesty's Performing Arts Centre side by side. As it should be, were he Aquarius. But he is not. He is merely Douglas.

No matter which side of this conflict they align, I know my fellows miss Aquarius. As do I. Aquarius has incarnated less and less over the millennia, and we feel the loss of one of our own.

But it is more than that, Aquarius was always the glue that held us together. A father. A son. A brother. Somehow, their unassuming yet forthwith nature has always appealed to each of us. At this time in particular, I yearn for Aquarius' input. More so than I yearn for that of Pisces. More so than I grieve the loss of Gemini. I *need* Aquarius, now. More than ever. With Aquarius by my side, endorsing the order, any consensus would be moot.

Instead, by my side is Douglas.

"Why are we at the theatre when there's not even a manta ray?"

"Matinee," I correct him.

He does not seem to understand the difference.

"We are here because Leo is rehearsing," I explain. "Though, he prefers to remain by the stage name; Leonardo Cantari."

Douglas nods. "Yep. Why not."

This flippant statement, more than any other display of ignorance, stops me in my stride. "You don't know who Leonardo Cantari is, do you?"

"Ye-ah," Douglas guffaws. "Of course I do." He indicates the doorway to the stage. "He's *Leo*. Duh."

With a restrained breath of frustration, I continue through the foyer. "Leonardo Cantari has regularly been acclaimed as the greatest operatic voice of the last century. He has performed for kings and dictators, brought hardened men to tears. More importantly, he is credited with opening the operatic world to the likes of *your* generation."

"Sounds to me like someone has a bit of a crush." The accompanying smirk Douglas wears is as ridiculous as his humour.

"Stop." I raise my arm so he is brought up short. "Listen."

Even from the lobby we can hear the epic voice as *Vesti La Giubba* begins. I take a moment to step outside myself and simply *enjoy* it. The pain. The tragedy. I have never seen the opera, though you would think I'd have managed to find the time over the last couple of centuries. But I know the aria well, have immersed myself in it, when I have had the time.

Eyes closed, I mouth the words. *'Tramuta in lazzi lo spasmo ed il pianto!'*—Turn into jokes, the spasms and tears. They seem so apt for these days.

Leo captures Canio's grief perfectly—the clown who must hide his grief and continue the show. I feel a deeper kinship with the words, now more than I ever have in the past. The strain impressed upon my body and mind from the Dawning; my murder of Taurus; the loss of Gemini, of Aquarius.

Libra.

My own grief passes, settling and fortifying my resolve. I take the lessons of Canio to heart—do not ignore your pain; use it. Transform it. The show must go on.

The plan must be adhered to.

When I open my eyes, Douglas is staring at me, his face a mix of confusion, wariness, and concern.

"Cap?" he asks. "You okay? Seem to have lost you for a moment, there."

How can I convey to him what has been sacrificed and lost? Aquarius would understand without the need to speak of it. But Douglas? Perhaps he would. For so long I have shunned human contact and been sentinel only—to the human race, to the needlessly short lives of my fellows, to the turning of the centuries. I had to. It was the only way to withstand the burden of millennia. To love is to lose, and I became tired of losing. But Douglas' concern has caught me off guard, and as I watch him now, in my moment of vulnerability, I realise my prison of isolation may not have been the salvation I thought it to be. Not truly.

To love is to lose. But, in time, is not all lost, regardless?

Is not salvation found in others?

I open my mouth to speak.

"Or maybe you're just geeking out over your man crush?" Douglas mocks.

My mouth closes again. No, there will be no salvation. Perhaps in others, but not in Douglas. My jaw tenses and I turn away.

The main stage of Her Majesty's was shrouded in darkness when Doug walked in with Capricorn. Though the house lights were off, Doug could clearly see the orchestra tending to their instruments with an air of discomfort as the voice of the great Leonardo Cantari boomed off the walls.

"I *will not* 'move with the light'," the thunder of his deep voice filled the hall. "The *light* should move with *me*!"

Seated in the third row, the stage manager removed her glasses and pinched the bridge of her nose. "We've been over this, Leonardo," she said in pained tones. "We don't have time for full tech and the tracking here isn't that sophisticated. We're having set choreography."

Even at this distance, Leo was a formidable and daunting presence. He was almost as wide as he was tall, a great hulk of a man adorned with dark, curling hair and a matching beard, although the former was streaked with the tell-tale grey of the Twelve. His legs, arms, and chest were massive, and even the great paunch about his middle spoke not of fat, but of *muscle*. Doug glanced at Capricorn as they waited in the shadows at the back of the theatre. Anxiety lapped at Doug that the *priomo uomo* would turn his eyes to their intrusion at any moment, and that fire and fury would follow.

"How can one *feel* the music if they're mired in *choreography*?" Leo spat the word as if it were foul. "Music is freedom! It is joyous rapture captured in sound! Performance should be a free expression of emotion!"

The stage manager sighed. "We're not going to have a repeat of Athens, are we?"

Leo.

Doug heard Capricorn's mental voice as clearly as if the word had been spoken. But it was more than hearing, he *felt* the voice inside of him. Tone, pitch, and intention were immediately clear to him in a way that was impossible with words alone. And, likewise, he *felt* Leo's queried response, though there was no voice attached to it.

"*Leave.*"

As the command reverberated around the room, Doug felt Capricorn grasp his arm, though there was no need. He felt no compulsion to obey, as he had done with Cancer. He marvelled at the stage manager, the orchestra, and the various techs and stagehands as they all turned and left the hall, as mindless as zombies.

"Still wishing to command every human around you, Leo?" Capricorn called as he made his way down the aisle.

Leo did not deign to leave the stage. "The humans are ours to command, Capricorn," he replied. "If you would only embrace the idea you could have fame and glory almost equal to my own."

Doug followed Capricorn up the stairs at the wing. He'd never been on a stage before, let alone one as grand as this. He didn't like the feeling. There was a nakedness that raised his blood pressure. He peered past the bright lights and into the darkness of the gallery, fearing the sudden appearance of an audience, but Leo's command had been absolute and they were alone.

"I'm not above the odd command," Capricorn said, waving a dismissive hand as he approached. "But my ego is not as fragile as yours, and I've gotten by just fine without manufacturing my successes."

The amber pits of Leo's eyes narrowed. "Choose your words carefully, Goat-Fish," he growled. "And remember to whom you speak."

Capricorn stood before Leo, and even his height was dwarfed by the man before him. "I am one of the Twelve and your equal. And I will speak to you in any manner I wish, *cub.*"

Leo's face hardened as he drew himself to his full height, bearing down on Capricorn, who stone-facedly met his stare. Doug tensed, ready to fight, or ready to run.

And then Leo laughed.

Leo's great arms wrapped around Capricorn, lifting him from his feet and crushing him to his chest as the vibrato of his laugh bounced off the walls, his face awash with a grin. But, more surprising than that, Capricorn responded in kind. There was no booming chuckle to accompany it, but he returned Leo's embrace, and the smile that lit his features washed away his usual stern visage.

Doug couldn't understand why, but in that moment, he hated Leo.

"It's been too long, Capricorn! Too long," Leo boomed as he set Capricorn back on his feet. "When was the last time we saw each other?"

"It was before Athens, that's for certain," Capricorn replied.

"Ah, yes. Athens. That unmitigated disaster." Leo scratched at his dark beard and sat on a nearby stool, which bowed to take his weight. "Nearly destroyed my career."

"I wouldn't dwell on it," Capricorn advised. "As I understand it, you're back on top and doing well for yourself. As usual."

Doug's jaw clenched at the casual tone of Capricorn's banter. Was this the same man who had left him to die, not an hour ago? The same man who, that very morning, had assailed him with bolts of burning yellow fire? Whom Doug had stood with during the vain attempt to rescue Aries? Where was *his* laughter? Where was *his* warm smile of gratitude? His chest and stomach tightened and he couldn't remove the scowl from his face.

Leo perked up. "I have a wonderful idea! We open in three days, you shall be my guest!"

"Sorry," Doug spoke through gritted teeth. "We'll be busy."

Leo's gaze fell on him, as if seeing him for the first time. "Capricorn," he said. "I see you've gotten yourself a valet!"

"I don't know what that is, but I'm not that," Doug snapped.

Leo's amber eyes narrowed. "A very ill-tempered valet. Capricorn, perhaps you wish to teach this whelp some manners?"

"I'm Aquarius, you overgrown buffoon!"

Capricorn shot him a look, severe and warning; the change of his moods giving Doug whiplash. Had he really just said that? Not the overgrown buffoon bit—*that* he felt was justified, though not his best insult ever. Had he just called himself Aquarius? Laid claim to that which had been thrust upon him?

He wished he could take it back.

Leo's gaze was penetrating as he rose from the stool to his full height. Doug thought he should be used to that look by now; the one that ignored Doug and sought only Aquarius. He'd endured it enough in the last two days. This time, though, it caused him to bristle.

"No," Leo said, his voice low and dark. "I can see the measure of Aquarius within you, but you are not Aquarius. You are a *whelp*. A little dandy boy. And I cannot fathom that Aquarius would be low enough to incarnate as *you*."

Capricorn's warning laced through his head, swift and fierce as lightning. *Protect yourself.*

Doug raised his arms in time to deflect the golden light of Leo's emanation. What the hell was it with these guys and attacking him? Doug bared his teeth and thrust his hand towards Leo, summoning the corposant blue-flame of his own emanation.

Except that nothing happened.

"You've got to be *kidding me!*" Doug screeched, and he dove to the side to avoid another blast from Leo.

He's testing you. He's not trying to hurt you, Capricorn said, whisper-quiet in the back of his brain. *Relax. Trust yourself and it will become natural.*

Doug grasped a music stand, the sheets tumbling to the floor. *I don't need your help!* he yelled back and raised his newfound weapon. With a roar of defiance, he launched himself at Leo, brandishing the music stand like a pike.

The hulk of a man batted it away, but Doug swung it around again and caught Leo in the chin.

Once, in year eight, Doug had stood up to the schoolyard bully—Jamie Thomas. Sick of the harassment and teasing, he'd thrown his backpack right into Jamie Thomas' smug face. But he'd not thrown it with enough force, and the black eye Jamie had given him in return lasted for three weeks.

The look on Leo's face would've made Jamie Thomas wet himself.

"Oh shi—"

The monster of a man lifted Doug with one hand and threw him across the stage.

You've been dallying, Capricorn. Leo's voice flooded Doug's head, with greater acoustics than any sound stage. *I've already been visited by Sagittarius.*

Capricorn disappeared from sight, and resolidified in front of Doug—arms spread, hands flaring. A physical barrier between himself and Leo.

Leo roared with laughter.

"Don't be so dramatic, Capricorn!" he boomed. "That's *my* area of expertise. Stick to your clandestine hoodwinkery."

Doug stood and tried to push past Capricorn, but the demigod held firm. "You betray Capricorn and you betray all of us!" he shouted. "I'll—err . . . I'll emanate you into the next Dawning!"

He felt, more than heard, Capricorn's sigh of frustration.

"Douglas, relax," he muttered.

"Fear not, whelp," Leo said, his great lips turned up in a wry smile. "I agree fervently with Capricorn's design. I sent Sagittarius to bed without any supper. But you," he said, waggling a sausage-sized finger at Doug, "you have *spirit*. Perhaps I like the dandy-boy, after all."

Doug felt a warm glow at Leo's endorsement. A glow he immediately quashed.

Capricorn lowered his arms. "So you will side with us at the Dawning?"

"Of course!" Leo bellowed. "Sagittarius is an impertinent upstart. She had her Age, it is time for Aquarius." He turned wistful. "Then we can all go home."

"Thank you, Leo," Capricorn said. "I presume that Virgo is with you, as always?"

"Yes, yes. Backstage and downstairs. Costuming, I believe."

Capricorn gave a sharp nod and left the stage, Doug turned to follow.

"Aquarius," Leo called to him. Hesitantly, Doug turned back. Leo gave him a warm smile. "Well done."

"I'll um . . ." Doug wasn't sure how to respond. "I'll see you . . . at . . . the thing . . ." he finished.

When he caught up with Capricorn the man was already on the stairs, descending into the bowels of the grand theatre.

"What did Leo mean about going home?" Doug asked. "Is this the last Age? Will you guys all be leaving once the Dawning is over?"

Capricorn's brow furrowed. "No, that's not part of the plan. I don't know what Leo meant."

They reached the bottom of the stairs. "Cancer said 'remember Thálassélas'," Doug told him. "What's Thálassélas?"

Capricorn paused, his head turning to the side and his brow creasing deeper. "I don't know," he admitted.

Capricorn continued his search for Virgo. Somehow, at the moment, the demigod seemed more like a man than Doug had ever seen him. More fallible, more uncertain. Not the witch who had appeared in his flat the day before, but not the demon who had attacked him with fury this morning. A man. As lost in his thoughts as he was in the labyrinthine building.

Tentatively, silently—as he had felt Capricorn do before—Doug reached out.

Pisces?

The reply was immediate, and surprised. *Doug? Is that you?* There was a tremor of excitement. *You can speak! How wonderful!*

I wanted to ask you something, Doug replied. *What exactly happens to one of you guys when you've been incarnate for as long as Cap?*

The excitement was replaced by unease. It seemed almost as if he were not speaking to her, but connecting with her in a more fundamental way.

To be honest, Doug, we don't know. No one has been incarnate for as long as Capricorn.

Doug sidestepped discarded cables and stage lights. *You said incarnation puts a strain on the mind*, he pressed. *What kind of strain?*

The longer one is incarnate, the longer they are separated from the spiritual realm. The mind becomes more human, more stretched. A human mind cannot contain our being; the full wealth of knowledge we have, the dichotomy of our physical and spiritual form, the weight of our previous incarnations.

So, you could forget who you are? Doug extrapolated. *Because each incarnation is not who you are, it is only one expression? And you could become lost in that expression?*

Exactly! Now you're getting the hang of it.

Pisces, Doug asked. *Where do you guys come from?*

From the universe, silly.

No, that's not what I mean. Doug closed his eyes briefly, trying to organise his thoughts and follow Capricorn through the building. *I mean*, where *did you come from? Are you super evolved humans? Did you come from another planet?*

He felt the confusion in Pisces' pause, almost as if she didn't understand the question.

We came into being with the development of human consciousness, she told him. *When humans made the transition from an animal level of consciousness to one that reached out to the universe, we came into being as its guardians. We have been guiding humanity ever since.*

Doug took a moment to contemplate that statement. *And how long ago was that?*

Oh, about three million years ago.

What?!

Give or take.

Doug struggled to recall his biology lessons—too many years ago. *Pisces, that can't be right. Humans weren't even around three million years ago!*

Not according to your *history,* she replied. *I guess we just have a broader definition of what 'human' means.*

Doug grappled with that statement, and Pisces was generous enough to give him mental space. Three million years of human consciousness—predating the appearance of humanity itself. Did that diminish the human condition somehow? Doug didn't think so. It somehow made it more special, bringing humanity's long-extinct cousins and ancestors closer to them, creating a more continuous narrative for the human race. He idly wondered what else was hiding beyond the limits of history and archaeology.

Pisces, is this 'history' one of the things you'd be likely to forget if you remained incarnate too long?

Ah, Pisces intoned. *Is this why you're asking these things of me, and not Capricorn?*

Doug's gaze shifted to the man, who's hand was resting on the wall, his grey eyes scanning the hallway beyond them.

He can probably hear us, you know, Pisces continued. *Your proximity to him alone should mean he is aware of our conversation. And, I'm sorry, Doug, but you're not exactly experienced with this form of communication. I highly doubt our conversation is private.*

Doug pursed his lips. *I dunno . . . Let me try something.*

He watched Capricorn.

CRAZY-GOAT-FISH-SAYS-WHAT?

The older man stilled, then the grey eyes turned on him. "Are you finished?" he asked.

Doug knew Pisces could feel his embarrassment. "Yes," he mumbled. "Sorry, Cap," he quickly added. *Bye, Pisces.*

"Good," Capricorn said, and he held one finger to his lips.

They had stopped before a door, and voices could be heard beyond it.

Capricorn was waiting, his head tilted as he tried to fathom the words from within. Without warning, he grasped the handle and threw the door open, causing it to bang against the wall inside and ricochet back on its hinges.

Inside was a lithe and beautiful man. He spun to face them, and it was clear from the widening of his eyes and breaths that his paled skin was not from sudden shock, but from previous terror.

The man forced a dazzling smile.

"Capricorn!" he gasped. "What a lovely surprise!" He came forward, and his hand was still shaking as he gripped Doug's and shook it. "A pleasure to meet you, Douglas," he said.

"I am Virgo."

To be continued in the next edition of the Zodiac Series—

Virgo . . .

About the Author:

Helena McAuley tries to expand her horizons by reading a mix of fiction and non-fiction. At the moment she is reading one of each; a fiction book, and a dictionary so she can understand the fiction book.

This doesn't always pan out, because Helena also loves learning new words, and will end up reading the dictionary instead for hours.

'This is the Dawning' is a serialised debut that will be published throughout the ASF Zodiac series. What has Virgo so spooked? Tune in next month! Same Zodiac time, same Zodiac channel!

Helena can be found (mostly) twit-ing, (sometimes) insta-ing, and is (rarely) facebookified under the handle @thathmc

ABOUT AUSSIE SPECULATIVE FICTION

Aussie Speculative Fiction is a recently established group which was created to support and promote Australian speculative fiction writers.

Check out our links:

www.facebook.com/Aussiespeculativefiction/

www.twitter.com/aussiefiction

www.aussiespeculativefiction.com

www.books2read.com/rl/asf

ABOUT DEADSET PRESS

Deadset Press is the publishing imprint of Aussie Speculative Fiction—a community aimed at supporting Australian and Kiwi authors. You can learn more at:

www.aussiespeculativefiction.com

ALSO BY DEADSET PRESS

<u>Annual Anthologies</u>

Beginnings: Aussie Speculative Fiction Anthology Vol. 1

Journeys: Aussie Speculative Fiction Anthology Vol. 2

\#

<u>Drowned Earth</u>

Prequel: Shards of Silver by Alanah Andrews

The Rise by Sue-Ellen Pashley

Fire Over Troubled Water by Nick Marone

Submerged City by Austin P. Sheehan

Tides of War by Marcus Turner

The Jindabyne Secret by Jo Hart

River of Diamonds by S. M. Isaac

Salvaged by C.A. Clark

Emoto's Promise by Shel Calopa

\#

<u>The Zodiac Series</u>

Capricorn (The Zodiac Series #1)

Aquarius (The Zodiac Series #2)

Pisces (The Zodiac Series #3)

Aries (The Zodiac Series #4)

Taurus (The Zodiac Series #5)